ATTACK OF THE CLONES™

A galaxy of reading . . .

Episode I: The Phantom Menace

Episode II: Attack of the Clones

Episode III: Revenge of the Sith

Episode IV: A New Hope

Episode V: The Empire Strikes Back

Episode VI: Return of the Jedi

THE LAST OF THE JEDI

The Desperate Mission

Dark Warning

Underworld

Death on Naboo

A Tangled Web

Return of the Dark Side

Secret Weapon

Against the Empire

Master of Deception

Reckoning

STAR WARS®

EPISODE II

ATTACK OF THE CLONES™

Patricia C. Wrede

Based on the story by George Lucas and the screenplay
by George Lucas and Jonathan Hales

SCHOLASTIC INC.

New York Toronto London Auckland Sydney
Mexico City New Delhi Hong Kong Buenos Aires

www.starwars.com
www.starwarskids.com
www.scholastic.com

ISBN-13: 978-0-439-13928-1
ISBN-10: 0-439-13928-7

Cover art by Louise Bova and Lucasfilm.

28 27 26 25 24 23 22 15 16/0

Printed in the U.S.A.
First Scholastic printing, May 2002

ATTACK OF THE CLONES™

PROLOGUE

A long time ago in a galaxy far, far away . . .

For generations, the Jedi Knights had kept peace among the many worlds of the Galactic Republic. They did not make the laws — that was the task of the Galactic Senate. The Jedi merely enforced them. Sometimes they negotiated; sometimes they used their awesome fighting skills; sometimes they used the mysterious power of the Force. Their methods had been extremely effective. For a thousand generations, there had been no major war in the galaxy. Only a few planets had experienced severe conflicts.

One of these planets was the small, watery world of Naboo. During an argument over taxing trade routes, the powerful Trade Federation landed a huge droid army on Naboo. The recently elected Queen of Naboo, young Padmé Amidala, refused to surrender. Her heroism and the efforts of the Jedi brought a quick end to the conflict, but many of the Naboo people had been hurt or killed.

The experience left a strong impression on Padmé. When she finished her two terms of office as Queen, she did not retire from politics. Instead, at the urging of the new Queen, she ran for the office of Galactic Senator, and became Naboo's representative. In the Senate, she was a strong voice for peace.

Such a voice was much needed. The Senate had become large and choked with bureaucracy. Many people were frustrated; some even talked of leaving the Republic and forming their own government. These Separatists were not a serious threat until Count Dooku, a former Jedi Knight, brought them together under his leadership.

The Separatist movement made it difficult for the limited number of Jedi Knights to continue to maintain peace. As the Jedi's task grew harder, more and more star systems joined the Separatists. Many in the Senate feared that if the Separatists refused to see reason, there would be war — and everyone knew that there were too few Jedi to keep the peace. For the first time in a thousand generations the Senate had to vote on whether to create an army.

Tension rose as those who feared the chaos caused by the Separatists clashed with those who feared that creating an army would destroy all hope for peace. Senator Padmé Amidala was one of the leaders fighting to prevent the creation of an army. Her passion and her commitment to peace, strengthened during the brief invasion of Naboo ten years earlier, made her arguments very convincing when she spoke to the Senate. More than one of the Senators who favored creating an army would have been glad to see Padmé disappear for good.

Padmé knew the danger, but her sense of duty was strong, and her love of peace was stronger. As the time for the final decision drew near, she headed for Coruscant to cast her vote against the Military Creation Act.

Senator Padmé Amidala stared out the main window of her spacecraft at the approaching planet. *Even from space, Coruscant looks different from other worlds,* she thought. Most worlds showed colors on their daylight side — the greens of the forest worlds, the blues of watery planets, the glittering white of ice worlds, the sandy yellow of desert planets like Tatooine. On their night side, most planets were dark, with an occasional twinkle of light marking the largest cities.

Coruscant's day side was a dull, metallic gray, the color of the millions of buildings and platforms that covered its entire surface. Its night side glowed amber from the lights of those same buildings, like the stars of the galaxy in miniature. *Only on Coruscant is night more attractive than day,* Padmé thought.

The royal Naboo cruiser and its three fighter escorts curved around Coruscant toward their assigned landing platform. Padmé hadn't wanted the escorts, but her security officer had insisted that she was in danger. Captain Typho was good at his job, so she had reluctantly agreed. Since the trip had been uneventful, she already regretted giving in.

The three lobes of the landing platform came in sight. The royal cruiser landed on the center leaf. The three fighters took the other leaves, two to one side and one to the other. Captain Typho, who had been piloting one of the fighters, swung out of his cockpit and removed his helmet.

"We made it," he said. "I guess I was wrong; there was no danger at all."

Padmé hardly heard him. On the platform, she could see Dormé, one of her handmaiden-bodyguards, waiting among the landing crew. Dormé looked tired and tense. *She's just worried,* Padmé thought. *She can't know how easy the trip was.*

The cruiser's ramp lowered. Padmé's guards came down first, then the rest of the Senatorial party. As they reached the foot of the ramp, the ground crew watched their arrival.

In the next instant, something knocked Padmé flat. Through the roaring in her ears, she heard cries of terror. She choked and blinked to clear the dark afterimage from her eyes — the image of the royal cruiser exploding. *Captain Typho was right after all,* she thought, and then, *Cordé! Is Cordé all right?*

She was still a little breathless from her fall, but she could not wait. She shoved herself to her feet and ran toward the wreckage. At the foot of the ramp lay several crumpled figures; one was Cordé, the decoy double who had been pretending to be Senator Amidala . . . pretending much too successfully for her own good.

Padmé ripped off her pilot's helmet and gathered Cordé in her arms. "Cordé . . ."

Cordé's eyes opened. She stared blankly at Padmé for an instant, then seemed to recognize her. "I'm sorry, M'lady," she gasped weakly. "I'm . . . not sure I . . . I've failed you, Senator."

Failed? No! But before she could speak the words, Padmé felt the life leave Cordé. She gathered her decoy's body close, as if she could call her back by sheer force of will. "No," she whispered. "No!" *Not now, not here, not when we were safe on Coruscant.*

But Coruscant was not safe. Captain Typho had thought that any attack would come during the trip, when an assassin would have all of space in which to flee. That was why he had insisted that Padmé pilot one of the fighters instead of relying solely on her double. "A decoy is no help if you're standing right next to it," he'd told her. "As long as you're on board, anyone who attacks the cruiser will attack you, even if Cordé is playing the Senator. You have to be somewhere else." So she had been, and now Cordé had died, just when they should all have been able to stop worrying at last.

As if in echo of her thoughts, Padmé heard Captain Typho's voice beside her saying urgently, "M'lady . . . you are still in danger here."

Gently, Padmé lowered Cordé — Cordé's body — to the ground. She looked up and saw other motionless bodies: two of her guards, another handmaiden. She swallowed hard and forced her eyes to move onto the twisted wreckage of the starship. *The cruiser's pilot was still on board, and others . . . how many others?* Tears stung her eyes. "I shouldn't have come back," she murmured, half to herself.

"This vote is very important," Typho reminded her. "You did your duty — and Cordé did hers. Now come."

Padmé hesitated, blinking the tears away. The least she could do was to see these people clearly, these people who had given their lives for her. *I will not let their sacrifice be in vain*, she promised silently. *There* WILL *be peace.*

"Senator Amidala, please!"

Captain Typho's voice sounded desperate as well as urgent. He was right again; she should go. Padmé took a last look around, printing the picture of the wreckage on her memory. Then she turned and fell into step beside him. Behind her, she heard a small whimpering noise from her faithful droid, R2-D2, but she did not turn. She had work to do.

It took longer than Padmé had expected to change and get to the Senate chamber. By the time she and her escorts arrived, most of the flying platforms that covered the walls of the vast arena were occupied and the session had started. Padmé heard one of the Senators shouting as she entered her platform.

". . . needs more security now! Before it comes to war."

Padmé craned her neck. The speaker was Orn Free Taa, the fat, blue-skinned Twi'leck Senator who was one of the biggest supporters of the Military Creation Act.

"Must I remind the Senator that negotiations are continuing with the Separatists?" Chancellor Palpatine said firmly. Padmé found it hard to understand how he could remain so calm in the face of such constant provocation, but somehow Palpatine always seemed unaffected by the angry shouting around him. "Peace is our objective here," the Chancellor went on, "not war."

As the Senators shouted responses to the Chancellor's comments, Padmé flicked the controls of her platform, setting it in motion. Deftly, she maneuvered around the other platforms already hovering near the center of the arena. As she passed them, she noted the occupants of the other pods — Ask Aak of Malastare, Darsana of Glee Anselm, and, of course, Orn Free Taa, all supporters of the bill. It was a good thing she had arrived when she did.

"My noble colleagues, I concur with the Supreme Chancellor!" Padmé said as soon as she reached the speaking area. "At all costs, we do not want war!"

To Padmé's surprise, a stunned silence fell over the entire Senate. A moment later, cheers and applause sounded from every platform. Even Orn Free Taa and Ask Aak joined in, though with less enthusiasm.

"It is with great surprise and joy that the chair recognizes the Senator from Naboo, Padmé Amidala," said Chancellor Palpatine. The unusual emotion in his voice told Padmé what had happened.

They must have heard about the explosion, Padmé thought. Well, perhaps she could use the attack to show them just how important this bill was. "Less than an hour ago, an assassination attempt was made against my life," she began. "One of my bodyguards and six others were ruthlessly and senselessly murdered." Her voice wavered as she remembered Cordé, but she forced herself on. She *must* show them how important it was to avoid war.

"I was the target," Padmé continued, "but more important I believe this security measure before you was the target. I have led the opposition to build an army . . . but there is someone in this body who will stop at nothing to assure its passage."

Some of the Senators booed. Padmé kept her face calm with the skill of long practice, but inwardly she was dismayed to see how many of her colleagues were slipping toward supporting the army bill. "I warn you," she said, "if you vote to create this army, war will follow. I have experienced the misery of war firsthand; I do not wish to do it again.

"Wake up, Senators!" Padmé cried over the rising shouts from other platforms. "You must wake up! If we offer the Separatists violence, they can only show us violence in return!" With growing passion, she pleaded with the Senators to reject the "security measure," but the response was a chorus of groans and boos.

Orn Free Taa moved his platform next to hers and addressed the Chancellor. "My motion to defer the vote must be dealt with first. That is the rule of law."

Padmé glared at him. From the central podium, Chancellor Palpatine gave her a sympathetic look, but his voice was as firm as it had been when he rebuked Ask Aak earlier. "Due to the lateness of the hour and the seriousness of this motion we will take up these matters tomorrow. Until then, the Senate stands adjourned."

What is he doing? Padmé thought as she maneuvered her platform back toward its docking place. *Is he so sure that we will lose the vote?*

A small viewscreen on the platform pinged, announcing a message. Padmé looked down. The

Chancellor was asking her to a private meeting in his office. Perhaps she would get some answers there.

Chancellor Palpatine's office, high in a skyscraper overlooking the Senate building, was vast but comfortable. The deep-cushioned blue sofa that faced the Chancellor's desk was wide enough and low enough to accommodate almost any life-form in the Republic with ease. Thick rugs covered the floor; tall windows let in light from every direction. The two royal guards, flanking the door in their new red robes and helmets, stood out against the soothing background, a reminder of both the power and the danger of the Chancellor's position.

Yoda approved of the windows, but the rest failed to impress him. Earned it, the Chancellor certainly had — no one could say he had not worked hard for the Republic and for peace. But Jedi preferred simpler surroundings, though none of the senior members of the Jedi Council who had come to discuss the situation with Chancellor Palpatine would ever have said so. The luxury made Yoda's ears twitch.

"I don't know how much longer I can hold off the vote, my friends," the Chancellor told the four Jedi facing him. His soft voice sounded tired. "More and more star systems are joining the Separatists."

And the Senators grew more afraid, and the more fearful they grew, the worse the situation became. *Fear feeds the dark side*, Yoda thought sadly. The clearest example of the spreading chaos was the explosion of Senator Amidala's space cruiser. *Seen it, we should have — seen it and prevented it.* But the Jedi had not seen, and now many lives had been lost and the fear among the Senators grew as the Separatists threatened to break away and perhaps start a civil war.

"If they do break away —" Mace Windu began reluctantly.

"I will not let this Republic that has stood for a thousand years be split in two!" Palpatine interrupted. "My negotiations will not fail!"

Afraid, the Chancellor is not, Yoda thought. He could sense the fearful emotions of the Senators, reflected in the Force, even at a distance. But from Palpatine he felt nothing but determination and confidence. Yet everyone knew that the Chancellor's best efforts had only delayed the Military Creation Act, not stopped it.

Mace Windu looked at Palpatine with a grave expression, and continued where he had left off. "But *if* they do, you must realize there aren't enough Jedi to protect the Republic. We are keepers of the peace, not soldiers." Beside him, Ki-Adi-Mundi nodded agreement.

Palpatine stared at them for a moment, then turned. "Master Yoda, do you think it will really come to war?"

Yoda closed his eyes and folded his long, flexible

ears down, the better to feel the future shifting of the Force. The dark side hung like a thick fog over everything, hiding even the near events that usually were so clear, and growing more dense the further ahead he tried to look. Lightsabers flashed blue and green in the fog, but few, too few, and he caught more and more glimpses of a glowing red that no Jedi would ever wield. "Worse than war, I fear," he murmured. "Much worse."

"What?" Palpatine demanded.

"What do you sense, Master?" Mace Windu asked almost simultaneously.

"The dark side clouds everything," Yoda said, shaking his head. "Impossible to see, the future is. But this I am sure of —" He opened his eyes. "Do their duty, the Jedi will."

The other Jedi looked at him, considering, while Palpatine turned to answer a buzzer on his desk. Yoda looked back, unsmiling. He had seen the Republic weather many crises during his near nine hundred years as a Jedi, but this one — this one was different. Never had the dark side felt so strong.

The office door opened. Even before the delegation of loyalist Senators entered, Yoda felt a familiar presence. Smiling a little sadly, he rose and moved forward to greet Senator Padmé Amidala. It was like her to insist on returning to work at once, despite the attempt on her life and the deaths among her crew.

Though her face was calm, Yoda could sense her grief. He spoke directly to it. "Padmé, your tragedy on the landing platform, terrible."

Padmé gave a tiny nod, as if she could not bear to speak.

"With you, the Force is strong, young Senator," Yoda went on, tapping her lightly with his cane. "To see you alive brings warm feelings to my heart."

"Thank you, Master Yoda," Padmé replied softly. She looked up at the other Jedi and asked, "Do you have any idea who was behind this attack?"

"Our intelligence points to disgruntled spice miners on the moons of Naboo," Mace Windu told her.

Padmé frowned. "I don't wish to disagree, but I think that Count Dooku was behind it."

Even Padmé's security officer looked startled by this announcement; apparently the young Senator had not told him of her theory. The other Senators murmured among themselves, except for Bail Organa, who studied Padmé thoughtfully. Mace Windu and Ki-Adi-Mundi exchanged glances. Then Mace said gently, "You know, M'lady, Count Dooku was once a Jedi. He wouldn't assassinate anyone. It's not in his character."

"In dark times, nothing is what it appears to be," Yoda put in before the young Senator could say anything rash. He looked at his colleagues and twitched his ears reprovingly. They should know better than to make assumptions, and in any case, this was no time to start an argument about the character of a former Jedi. Besides, they were drifting from the most important point. "The fact remains for certain, Senator: in grave danger you are."

Padmé's frown deepened. Chancellor Palpatine studied her for a moment, then rose and went to the window. Looking out over the city, he said, "Master Jedi, may I suggest that the Senator be placed under the protection of your graces?"

"Do you think that is a wise decision during these stressful times?" Bail Organa asked, glancing at Padmé.

"Chancellor," Padmé said, sounding slightly put out, "if I may comment, I do not believe the situation —"

"— is that serious." Chancellor Palpatine picked up the sentence and finished it for her. "No, but I do, Senator."

"Chancellor, please!" Padmé looked appalled. "I don't want any more guards!"

The Chancellor gave her a mildly reproving glance. "I realize all too well that additional security might be disruptive for you, but perhaps someone you are familiar with . . ." He paused for a moment, his expression thoughtful. Then he smiled. "An old friend, like . . . Master Kenobi?" He nodded inquiringly at Mace Windu.

"That's possible," Mace replied slowly. "He has just returned from a border dispute on Ansion."

"You must remember him, M'lady," Palpatine said, turning back to Padmé. "He watched over you during the blockade conflict."

"This is not necessary, Chancellor!" Padmé insisted.

"Do it for me, M'lady, please," Palpatine almost begged. "I will rest easier. We had a big scare today. The thought of losing you is unbearable."

Padmé sighed and nodded.

"I will have Obi-Wan report to you immediately, M'lady," Mace Windu said gravely. He and Ki-Adi-Mundi rose to leave.

Yoda paused before following them. Something more was needed. He studied Padmé, who was biting her lip in evident frustration, then leaned in close to her ear. "Too little about yourself you worry, Senator, and too much about politics."

Padmé looked at him, startled. Yoda smiled slightly. "Be mindful of your danger, Padmé. Accept our help."

As they left the Chancellor's office, Yoda was pleased to see Padmé looking thoughtful instead of annoyed. Her heart was good, but too often did she act on impulse. Better she would do if she stopped to think, and let wisdom guide her passion.

The hydrolift door slid open, letting in a wash of cool, damp air. *Of course,* thought Anakin. *Padmé has set the climate to feel like Naboo.* In the past ten years, he had grown accustomed to worlds that were too cold and too damp — after growing up on Tatooine, nearly everywhere else felt too cold and too damp to him. But *this* damp cold was different. It reminded him of his first spaceship flight, aboard the royal Naboo cruiser, when Padmé had found him shivering in the main room in the middle of the night. She had covered him with her overjacket . . . he could still remember the faint scent on the red silk. He shook himself and followed Master Obi-Wan out of the lift.

Anakin had been hoping that Padmé would be there to greet them, but the only person in sight was Jar Jar Binks. The Gungan's long orange earflaps hung down over his robes, but Jar Jar's enthusiastic — and slightly awkward — greeting made it clear that his years in Galactic politics had not changed him much from the clumsy, confused Gungan Anakin remembered.

"It's good to see you, too, Jar Jar," Obi-Wan said, smiling in spite of himself.

"And dis is yousa apprentice," Jar Jar said, with an attempt at dignity. Then he peered more closely at Anakin. "Noooo! Annie? Noooo! Little bitty Annie? Yousa so biggen!"

"Hi, Jar Jar," Anakin said, grinning. He hoped the Gungan wasn't going to remind everyone of his childhood. Still, Jar Jar's happiness was irresistible, and he let himself be pulled into an enormous hug.

"Shesa expecting yousa," Jar Jar went on, and

Anakin's heart leaped. Jar Jar looked at him again, shook his head, and said, "Annie . . . mesa no be-lieven!"

When Jar Jar finished exclaiming over them, he led the way into a room off the main corridor. Anakin had a vague impression of light and under-stated elegance, but his attention was caught imme-diately by the sight of Padmé and one of her handmaidens conferring with a man wearing an eye patch and a Naboo captain's uniform.

Anakin stopped short. Light gleamed on the coils of Padmé's dark hair, and a long blue velvet vest clung to her slender figure. She was even more beau-tiful now than she had been at fourteen, even more beautiful than the rosy memory he had treasured for ten years. The thought that someone wanted to hurt her made his heart ache. He hardly heard Jar Jar say, "Lookie, lookie, Senator! Desa Jedi arriven."

Padmé and the others turned. When she saw Obi-Wan, Padmé smiled in recognition and rose to greet him. *She hardly even saw me,* Anakin thought.

"It's a pleasure to see you again, M'lady," Obi-Wan said.

Padmé smiled and took his hand. "It has been far too long, Master Kenobi. I'm so glad our paths have crossed again." She hesitated. "But I must warn you that I think your presence here is unnecessary."

Obi-Wan said only, "I'm sure the Jedi Council has their reasons."

Releasing Obi-Wan's hand, Padmé moved in front of Anakin. He looked down at her as she stared up doubtfully at him. Surely she remembered! Finally, she said hesitantly, "Annie??"

Anakin nodded. Padmé stared for another moment, then said weakly, "My goodness, you've grown."

"So have you," Anakin replied. *What a stupid thing to say, when I'm looking down at her!* "Grown more beautiful, I mean. And much shorter —" *Why did I have to say that? But it's so odd, when I remember her as so much taller than me.* "— for a Senator, I mean." *She's going to think I'm an idiot.*

Obi-Wan clearly thought so; the disapproving look he gave Anakin was all too familiar. But to his relief, Padmé only laughed and shook her head. Then she said, "Oh, Annie, you'll always be that little boy I knew on Tatooine."

Discomfited, Anakin looked down. *I'm not a little boy anymore!* He was almost glad when Obi-Wan distracted her, saying, "Our presence will be invisible, M'lady, I assure you."

"I'm very grateful you're here, Master Kenobi," the Naboo captain said. "The situation is more dangerous than the Senator will admit."

"I don't need more security," Padmé said firmly. "I need answers. I want to know who is trying to kill me."

"We're here to protect you, Senator, not to start an investigation," Obi-Wan said, frowning.

Anakin couldn't stand the look on her face. "We will find out who's trying to kill you, Padmé, I promise you!" he burst out.

Obi-Wan gave him another, even more disapproving look, and said sternly, "We are not going to exceed our mandate, my young Padawan learner."

"I meant in the interest of protecting her, Master, of course," Anakin replied. How could they keep her safe if they didn't know who was behind the assassination attempt? Surely Obi-Wan could see the need. If only he weren't always so determined to follow the rules. . . .

As if he had heard Anakin's thoughts, Obi-Wan shook his head. "We are not going through this exercise again, Anakin. And you will pay attention to my lead."

"Why?" Anakin persisted. He knew he was on dangerous ground, but this concerned Padmé.

"What??!!"

"Why else do you think we were assigned to her, if not to find the killer?" Anakin explained hastily. "Protection is a job for local security, not Jedi. It's overkill, Master. Investigation is implied in our mandate." At least this time Obi-Wan was listening.

"We will do as the Council has instructed," Obi-Wan said. "And you will learn your place, young one."

Anakin nodded, but he noticed that Obi-Wan had not repeated his statement that they were only supposed to act as guards. That was enough, for now. He could push more for the investigation later on. He would *make* Obi-Wan see.

"Perhaps with merely your presence, the mysteries surrounding this threat will be revealed," Padmé said, and Anakin was not sure whether she intended to be sarcastic or not. "Now, if you will excuse me, I will retire."

Anakin stared gloomily after Padmé and her handmaiden as Obi-Wan and the Naboo captain discussed security arrangements. The captain departed, leaving only Jar Jar, who was still burbling about how happy he was to see them. *Jar Jar isn't the one I wanted to feel happy*, Anakin thought, and immediately felt guilty. Jar Jar had a good heart. But . . .

"She didn't even recognize me, Jar Jar." The words slipped out before he realized. "I've thought about her every day since we parted, and she's forgotten me completely."

Jar Jar blinked at him, then said with surprising gentleness, "Shesa happy. Happier den mesa see-en her in longo time."

"Anakin, you're focusing on the negative again," Obi-Wan put in. "Be mindful of your thoughts. She was glad to see us. Now, let's check the security here."

It was something to do, and it would serve Padmé. Even if she didn't care whether or not he served her. "Yes, Master," said Anakin.

* * *

Zam Wesell pulled her speeder up to the side of the skyscraper and set the controls to hover. Her contact was already waiting for her, fully armed and armored. She snorted softly. Why Jango Fett made such a thing out of wearing that Mandoralian battle armor all the time, she couldn't understand. *I'm surprised he doesn't wear it when he's not on a job.*

She considered morphing into another form, just to annoy him. Changelings could pass for whatever race they chose; the ability was part of what made her such a successful bounty hunter. Fett could use the reminder, after the way his last little plan had gone wrong. She smiled behind the veil that hid the lower half of her face. She'd agreed to work with Fett on this, but she didn't have to keep him happy. On the other hand, they *did* have to work together. She decided not to waste the energy.

If Jango was having any similar thoughts about her, his helmet hid them. "We'll have to try something more subtle this time, Zam," he said without preamble as soon as she was close enough. "My client is getting impatient."

I'll bet, Zam thought, but she only nodded.

"There can be no mistakes this time," the other bounty hunter went on. "Take these. Be careful. They're very poisonous."

He reached out, offering her a short, fat tube. Through the clear sides, she saw several kouhuns —

foot-long creatures that looked like giant worms with hundreds of legs. She took the tube, her mind racing. Poisonous — she'd have to be sure the Senator was alone, and unlikely to notice their approach. Giving Jango an absentminded nod, she tucked her new assassination weapon under her arm and walked back to her airspeeder, lost in contemplation of the job ahead.

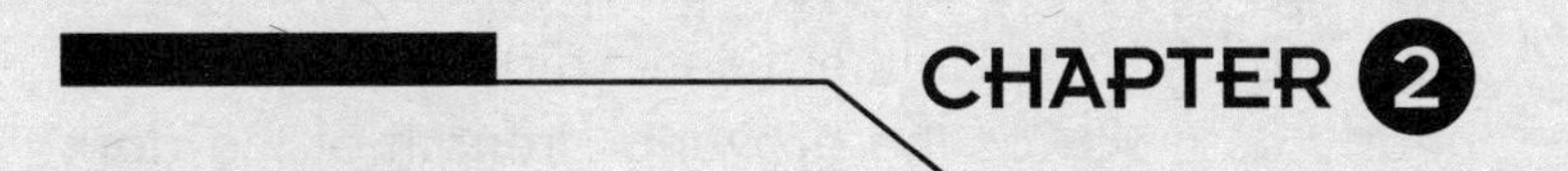

CHAPTER 2

The wide hallway near the center of the Jedi Temple was lit only by the light that seeped through the doorways at either end. Yoda had always liked the play of light against dark, but tonight, walking down the hallway with Mace Windu, it saddened him. Too much of the growing dark side, it reminded him.

Mace Windu broke the silence. "Why couldn't we see this attack on the Senator?" His deep voice was full of concern.

"Masking the future, is this disturbance in the Force," Yoda replied calmly.

"The prophecy is coming true," Windu said, frowning. "The dark side is growing."

Yoda nodded. "And only those who have turned to the dark side can sense the possibilities of the future." He could feel Mace's unquiet at his words, and he understood it well. A good part of the Jedi's remarkable success came from their ability to anticipate the future. The young ones had always relied on it — perhaps a little too much. Eight hundred years gave one a different perspective. The loss of their ability to see the future didn't worry Yoda nearly as much as the growing strength of the dark side that had caused the loss.

After a short silence, Mace said, "It's been ten years, and the Sith still have not shown themselves."

"Out there, they are," Yoda said, but he nodded in approval. Learned well the ways of the Force, Mace Windu had. He saw past his own concern to the heart of the real problem. "A certainty, that is."

Mace nodded, and they continued their walk toward the light in silence.

An eddy in the Force roused Anakin from his meditation. Someone was coming. Anakin's lightsaber leaped into his hands almost before his eyes opened; then, as he felt the presence more clearly, he smiled and replaced the weapon at his belt. It was only Obi-Wan, returning from his security check.

The door of Padmé's apartment slid open. "Captain Typho has more than enough guards downstairs," Obi-Wan said as he entered. "No assassin will try that way. Any activity up here?"

"Quiet as a tomb," Anakin replied without thinking, then shivered slightly at the phrase. He caught Obi-Wan's look, and answered the question his

Master had not asked aloud. "I don't like just waiting here for something to happen to her."

Obi-Wan nodded understandingly, and pulled a pocket viewscreen from his belt pack. A moment later, he frowned and held it up. The screen showed R2-D2, powered down, in a corner near the door of Padmé's bedroom, but there was no image of the bed, or of Padmé herself. "What's going on?" Obi-Wan asked.

Anakin shrugged. "She covered that camera. I don't think she liked me watching her."

"What is she thinking?" Obi-Wan said, shaking his head.

"She programmed Artoo to warn us if there's an intruder."

"It's not an intruder I'm worried about," Obi-Wan replied. "There are many other ways to kill a Senator."

"I know, but we also want to catch this assassin," Anakin said. "Don't we, Master?"

Obi-Wan's eyes widened. "You're using her as *bait*?"

"It was her idea," Anakin said defensively. She'd insisted, in fact. "Don't worry, no harm will come to her. I can sense everything going on in that room." Where Padmé was concerned, his normal sense of the Force was heightened; he could sense her breathing, if he tried. But he couldn't explain that to Obi-Wan. "Trust me."

"It's too risky," Obi-Wan said, frowning. "And your senses aren't that attuned, young apprentice."

Yes, they are! But Anakin had heard the faint extra emphasis on "*your* senses"; maybe Obi-Wan would let this go on, after all. "And yours are?"

"Possibly," said Obi-Wan. He made no move to wake Padmé, and Anakin suppressed a grin of satisfaction. They *would* get the assassin this way. After a moment, Obi-Wan said, "You look tired."

"I don't sleep well anymore," Anakin admitted.

"Because of your mother?" Obi-Wan asked gently.

"I don't know why I keep dreaming about her now," Anakin said. *Especially such awful dreams.* His mother was strong and gentle; his memories of her did not include menacing omens or threats. But his dreams did. He hunched his shoulders. "I haven't seen her since I was little."

"Dreams pass in time."

These hadn't. If anything, they were growing more frequent. But he didn't want to discuss it with Obi-Wan right now. Obi-Wan had never met Shmi Skywalker; he couldn't really understand. "I'd rather dream of Padmé," he said slyly, knowing it would distract his Master. "Just being around her again is . . . intoxicating."

"Be mindful of your thoughts, Anakin," Obi-Wan said sharply. "They betray you. You've made a commitment to the Jedi Order — a commitment not easily broken. And don't forget, she's a politician. They're not to be trusted."

"She's not like the others in the Senate, Master," Anakin said, stung by the unexpected criticism.

Obi-Wan shrugged. "It's been my experience that Senators are focused only on pleasing those who fund their campaigns — and they are more than willing to forget the niceties of democracy to get those funds."

"Not another lecture, Master," Anakin groaned. He found both politics and economics boring, and Obi-Wan would go on for hours once he got started. "Besides, you're generalizing. The Chancellor doesn't appear to be corrupt."

"Palpatine is a politician," Obi-Wan replied. "He's very clever at following the passions and prejudices of the Senators."

"I think he is a good man," Anakin said firmly. "My instincts are very positive about —" He broke off, stunned by a sudden feeling of menace radiating from Padmé's room. He glanced at his Master.

"I sense it, too," Obi-Wan said, and together they charged for the bedroom door.

Padmé! Anakin threw himself over the bed, his lightsaber humming through the air. Behind him, he heard the crash of breaking glass, but all his attention was concentrated on two kouhuns hissing on Padmé's pillow and flicking their stinger tongues. His swing passed a hair's breadth from Padmé's frozen face and sliced the deadly worms in half. *How did they get in here?*

Lightsaber still ready, Anakin turned. There was no sign of Obi-Wan, only the shattered bedroom window and the nighttime lights of buildings and flyers outside. Then Anakin saw a Probe Droid flying out into the city traffic, with his Master clinging grimly to two of its projections. His first thought was, *So that's how the kouhuns got in*; his second was, *But we're more than a hundred stories up! If he loses his grip . . .*

Anakin whirled. Padmé was sitting up in bed, her horrified eyes also fixed on the rapidly departing Assassin Droid. He could feel Captain Typho and his guards approaching; they could handle things here for the time being. He had to follow Obi-Wan. "Stay here!" he barked at Padmé, and ran out past Captain Typho and the guards, heading for the express elevator.

This was not the best idea I have ever had, Obi-Wan thought as he swung from the droid. But he hadn't expected it to take off the way it had. He certainly hadn't expected it to dodge into the heart of the speeder traffic, or to swing in and out in an attempt to get rid of him. Somebody had done a good job programming it.

The droid sent out an electric shock, and Obi-Wan almost lost his grip. Even the Force couldn't save him if he fell hundreds of stories. He grabbed at a wire on the back of the droid, and it came loose. The droid's power failed, and the electric shocks stopped . . . but so did the droid's antigravity. They dropped nearly thirty stories before Obi-Wan got the wire connected again. *Definitely not one of my best ideas.*

The wild ride continued. The droid knocked against walls, trying to scrape Obi-Wan off; swooped low over a roof; pulled into the hot exhaust stream of a speeder. Obi-Wan hung on. If he didn't capture the droid, they would have no clue to the assassin — and he didn't want to think about what Padmé and Anakin might come up with next time, if using her as bait failed!

The droid dropped toward an alcove in the side of a building, still high above the ground. Peering over its top, Obi-Wan saw a beat-up yellow airspeeder and a muffled figure in brown waiting in the alcove. The figure saw the approaching droid and pulled out a laser rifle. "I have a bad feeling about this," Obi-Wan muttered. A moment later, explosions burst all around the him. *If I could just use my lightsaber . . .* But he couldn't reach his weapon without letting go of the droid, and the minute he did that, the droid would find a way to throw him off. All he could do was hope that the assassin had very bad aim.

The assassin didn't. A shot hit the droid dead on. The explosion threw Obi-Wan up in the air — *Oh, great,* he thought hazily, *now I have farther to fall* — and away from the building, with nothing between him and the ground far below.

Half stunned, Obi-Wan saw a speeder approaching as he fell. He grabbed for it and barely caught the back end. As he hauled himself up to relative safety, he realized that the pilot was his apprentice.

"That was wacky!" Anakin said cheerfully as Obi-Wan reached the passenger seat and collapsed into it. "I almost lost you in the traffic."

Obi-Wan could sense the depth of the relief that Anakin wouldn't speak aloud. "What took you so long?" he said, knowing that Anakin would understand his unspoken thank-you in the same way.

"Oh, you know, Master, I couldn't find a speeder I really liked," Anakin said. "With an open cockpit, and the right speed capabilities . . . and then you know I had to get a really gonzo color . . ." As he spoke, he pulled the speeder into a steep climb, following the scruffy flyer who had been firing at Obi-Wan.

"If you'd spend as much time working on your saber skills as you do on your wit, young Padawan, you would rival Master Yoda as a swordsman," Obi-Wan told him.

"I thought I already did," Anakin said, grinning.

"Only in your mind, my very young apprentice . . . Careful!" Obi-Wan clutched at the side of the speeder as Anakin dodged rapidly in and out of the traffic. Shots flew past; the assassin was firing at them. "Hey, easy!"

"Sorry," Anakin said, whipping past a large commuter vehicle with almost no room to spare. "I forgot you don't like flying, Master."

"I don't mind flying," Obi-Wan said, "but what you're doing is suicide."

"I've been flying since before I could walk," Anakin said confidently, skimming by a commuter train almost close enough to scrape paint off the side of the speeder. "I'm very good at this."

It only takes one mistake. "Just slow down!"

Anakin paid no attention. The assassin tried to lose them in a convoy of huge freight vehicles, then zipped through several sharp turns into impossibly narrow spaces between buildings. Anakin followed every move.

"There he goes!" Obi-Wan said, pointing as the yellow speeder dove out of the traffic lane and around a corner. Then, as Anakin followed, Obi-Wan realized where the assassin was heading — straight into a tram tunnel. "Wait! Don't go in there!"

"Don't *worry*, Master," Anakin said soothingly . . . and sent the speeder into the tunnel right after the assassin.

He sounds as if he's humoring me, Obi-Wan thought. *But this is — oh, no!* The light just ahead wasn't the end of the tunnel; it was one of the giant passenger trams heading straight for them.

Barely in time, Anakin and the assassin whipped their speeders around and headed back the way they had come. They made it out of the tunnel just ahead of the high-speed tram. Obi-Wan let out a breath he had not realized he had been holding. "You know I don't like it when you do that," he commented.

"Sorry, Master," Anakin said unrepentantly. "Don't worry. This guy's going to kill himself any minute now."

Someone is going to get killed, Obi-Wan thought as the wild ride continued. *I hope it isn't us. . . .*

They rounded a corner, past a row of banners waving in the wind, and the near wing clipped one of the flags. The speeder lurched as the flag draped over its front end. "That was too close," Obi-Wan said.

"Clear that!" Anakin snapped.

"What?" For a moment, Obi-Wan did not understand; then he realized that the flag was blocking one of the air scoops. Without air, their engine was strangling. He leaned out of the speeder, but the flag was too far away to reach.

"Clear the flag!" Anakin struggled with the controls, scowling fiercely. "We're losing power! Hurry!"

There was only one thing to do. Obi-Wan crawled out onto the engine until he could reach the flag. He pulled it free — and the speeder lurched forward, regaining all the speed it had lost. The jerk almost made Obi-Wan lose his grip; he slid backward more than a meter before he caught himself.

"I don't like it when you do that," he complained as he crawled back into his seat.

"So sorry, Master," Anakin said, and this time Obi-Wan thought he really did mean it, at least a little. *But only a little.*

The incident with the flag had cost them time — the assassin's speeder was well ahead of them now. Anakin played his controls like a musician, narrowing the gap once more. *He was flying Podracers when he was barely a boy,* Obi-Wan thought, and shook his head. He reminded himself of that every time they got into one of these chases, and it never made him feel any better . . . because it also reminded him that Anakin had crashed every Podracer he had flown, except the last. *It's a wonder he survived. . . . What? Wait a minute!*

The assassin was heading straight for a power refinery. "It's dangerous near those power couplings!" Obi-Wan warned. "Don't go through there!"

But Anakin dove after the other speeder. The presence of the two vehicles triggered giant electric arcs; Obi-Wan's skin tingled with the nearness of their passage. "What are you *doing*?"

"Sorry, Master!"

Anakin sounded a little harried. Obi-Wan clamped his mouth shut over any further comments until they were out of the refinery. Then he said sarcastically, "Oh, that was good!"

"That was crazy," Anakin said flatly. His eyes were still fixed on the speeder ahead of them.

"I'm glad you agree" was on the tip of Obi-Wan's tongue. Then the other speeder twisted sideways and stopped in the mouth of an alley, firing at them point-blank.

"Stop!" Obi-Wan yelled. If they kept on this course, they would crash right into the other speeder — no, maybe not. There was an impossibly small gap just under the assassin's vehicle, and Anakin was aiming for it.

"We can make it," Anakin said, and the next minute they were under the assassin's ship. They made it through the gap, but hit a pipe on the other side and spun wildly. Anakin struggled to regain control. Obi-Wan saw a construction crane swing by, and a pair of supporting struts. He felt a jolt as the speeder brushed against something, and a giant gas ball enveloped them. The speeder spun, bumped against a building, and stalled.

Why do I always let him drive? "I'm crazy," Obi-Wan muttered, dropping his head onto his hands. "I'm crazy."

"I got us through that one all right," Anakin said in a satisfied tone.

Obi-Wan raised his head angrily. "No, you didn't! We've stalled. And you almost got us killed!"

"Oh, I think we're still alive," Anakin said absently as he fiddled with the controls. The engine coughed, then roared back to life, and he smiled.

The smile made Obi-Wan furious. Anakin wasn't even listening. "*It was stupid!*" he said.

His tone finally seemed to get through to his apprentice. Anakin blinked, then hung his head. "I *could* have caught him. . . ."

"But you didn't!" Obi-Wan glared at Anakin. "And now we've lost him for good!"

Suddenly an explosion rocked the speeder. Obi-Wan ducked, hearing the unmistakable *pzing* of laser bolts striking nearby.

"No, we haven't," Anakin said, and Obi-Wan felt the speeder lean sideways as Anakin tried to get them out of the ambush.

CHAPTER 3

Through the smoke and flames, Anakin saw their quarry take off into the night traffic. He sent the speeder roaring after it, but with less enthusiasm than before. This chase was getting them nowhere. The yellow speeder pulled down and left, and disappeared between two buildings. Anakin smiled and pulled away to the right. He had an idea. *Now, if he just goes where I think . . .*

"Where are you going?" Obi-Wan demanded. "He went down there, the other way."

His Master was still angry about the stall. Anakin sighed. "Master, if we keep this chase going, that creep is going to end up deep-fried. Personally, I'd very much like to find out who he is and who he's working for. This is a shortcut." He paused, then added honestly, "I think."

"What do you mean, you *think*?" Obi-Wan paused, waiting. When Anakin didn't react to his sarcasm, he repeated, "Well, you lost him."

Anakin brought the speeder to a halt, hovering halfway up between two giant buildings. "I'm deeply sorry, Master," he said absently. Trying to explain now would just mean more argument; there wasn't time. Obi-Wan would understand when . . . He saw the movement he had been waiting for, and began counting to himself.

"Some shortcut," Obi-Wan muttered. "He went completely the other way. Anakin —"

"Excuse me for a moment," Anakin interrupted, and jumped out of the speeder and into the air.

He had timed it perfectly; their scruffy quarry was several stories below, and Anakin landed on the roof of the yellow speeder. Before he could find a handhold, the pilot gunned the engines and Anakin nearly slid off. Then, as he clawed his way forward, the assassin brought the vehicle to an abrupt stop. Anakin flew forward. He grabbed one of the front forks of the speeder just in time. The assassin started firing at him.

Anakin dodged the first few bolts, then found a position that shielded him from the attack. The assassin took off again. A quick glance upward told Anakin that Obi-Wan had taken over the controls of the other speeder and was gaining on them. *Good; this guy has two things to worry about now.*

Slowly, Anakin worked his way back to the roof of the speeder. Pulling out his lightsaber, he began melting his way inside. A shot from inside the speeder knocked the lightsaber out of his hand. *I bet I hear about that from Master Obi-Wan,* Anakin thought gloomily, ducking another shot as the lightsaber fell away below them. *But first I have to get that blaster away from this guy.* The hole he'd started melting in the roof wasn't large enough to climb through, but there was plenty of room for his arm. He shoved his hand into the cockpit and snatched at the pistol, using the Force to help.

The assassin jerked, startled, and looked up. For just an instant, a woman's eyes stared at Anakin. *Hey, that guy isn't a guy! They sent a woman to assassinate Padmé!* Anakin reached out with the Force to confirm his observation, and felt an unusual quiver. *She's female, but she's not as human as she looks. A shape-changer?* Sure enough, the assassin changed again into Clawdite. Distracted, Anakin's grip on the blaster slipped. The pistol went off, blowing a hole in the floor of the speeder.

The speeder dove toward the street, out of control. All Anakin could do was hang on. At the last minute, the assassin pulled the nose up just enough to slide the speeder to a hard landing. Sparks showered everywhere, and people dodged out of the way. Anakin flew over the front of the speeder and landed in the street.

That woman is nearly as good a pilot as I am, Anakin thought. He picked himself up in time to see the assassin jump out of the wrecked speeder and run up the street. He followed, shoving through a rapidly growing crowd of seedy-looking aliens and scruffy droids. *Reminds me of Tatooine . . .*

Anakin was gaining steadily on the assassin now, but suddenly she ducked through the door of a nightclub, the Outlander. Panting slightly, Anakin reached the nightclub door just as another speeder came in for a much less spectacular landing. Obi-Wan climbed out, holding Anakin's lightsaber. *Uh-oh. I* knew *I was going to hear about that.*

"Anakin!" said Obi-Wan.

"She went into that club, Master," Anakin said, trying to distract him.

"Patience," Obi-Wan told him. "Use the Force, Anakin. Think."

"Sorry, Master," Anakin said automatically. Think? He thought the assassin was getting away. Surely Obi-Wan could see —

Obi-Wan sighed. "He went in there to hide, not run."

Oh. "Yes, Master," Anakin said.

Obi-Wan held out the lightsaber. "Here. Next time, try not to lose it."

That wasn't so bad. Anakin nodded and reached for the weapon.

Obi-Wan pulled it back. "A Jedi's saber is his most precious possession."

"Yes, Master." He wasn't going to escape the lecture after all. He reached for the sword again, and Obi-Wan pulled it away once more.

"He must keep it with him at all times," Obi-Wan said.

"I *know*, Master," Anakin said.

"This weapon is your life."

Anakin barely kept from rolling his eyes. "I've heard this lesson before."

"But you haven't learned anything, Anakin." Obi-Wan held the lightsaber out at last, and Anakin grabbed it before he could change his mind.

"I try, Master."

Obi-Wan sighed and turned toward the nightclub. "Why do I think you are going to be the death of me?" he said almost absently.

A chill ran down Anakin's spine. "Don't say that, Master!" he burst out, careless of the crowd who might overhear. Obi-Wan looked at him and lifted his eyebrows in a combination of question and reproof. Anakin swallowed and continued in a lower tone, "You're the closest thing I have to a father. I love you. I don't want to cause you pain." *I don't want to lose you, the way I've lost my mother.* Remembering his dreams, Anakin shivered. Would he start having nightmares about Obi-Wan, too?

But Obi-Wan only looked at him and said mildly, "Then why don't you listen to me?"

"I *am* trying."

Obi-Wan nodded. He glanced out over the crowded room and said in the same, almost-lecturing tone, "Do you see him?"

"I think he's a she," Anakin said. Rapidly, he scanned the crowd, but he did not see anyone who looked like their quarry. Remembering the strangeness he had sensed, he added, "And I think she's a changeling."

"Then be extra careful," Obi-Wan said. Anakin blinked in surprise, and his Master nodded gently toward the room. "Go and find her."

"But — but where are you going, Master?" Anakin said as Obi-Wan moved off into the crowd.

"To get a drink," Obi-Wan said over his shoulder.

Anakin blinked again, then began working his way around the edge of the room. Beings of all sorts stared at him, then looked away; most were too large or too small, or had too many appendages, to be the assassin. *Obi-Wan must be really worried,* he thought with the corner of his mind that wasn't hunting for the assassin. It wasn't like his Master to leave Anakin to do the work, but perhaps . . . Anakin glanced back toward the bar and saw the assassin at last — standing right behind Obi-Wan with a blaster in one hand.

Before Anakin could shout a warning, Obi-Wan whirled. His lightsaber hummed across the sudden silence, slicing through the assassin's arm. Anakin headed toward the bar. He could sense the assassin's pain and the growing anger of the beings around him, but his Master felt calm and centered, as always. *He expected this to happen,* Anakin thought indignantly. *He set himself up as bait!* Then he was at Obi-Wan's side. The assassin lay in a heap at Obi-Wan's feet. The assassin's arm — and blaster — lay in a pool of blood a little to one side.

"Easy," Anakin told the crowd. "Official business. Go back to your drinks."

Slowly, the bar patrons complied; apparently two lightsabers were more than any of them cared to face, especially with one person already in pieces. Obi-Wan snapped off his lightsaber; a moment later, Anakin did the same. Together, they carried the injured assassin outside.

"Do you know who it was you were trying to kill?" Obi-Wan asked as he tended her shoulder.

"The Senator from Naboo," the assassin replied readily.

"Who hired you?"

The woman glared at Obi-Wan, and Anakin thought that she was not going to tell them anything more. Then she said, "It was just a job. And the next one won't make the same mistake I did."

"Tell us!" Anakin demanded, pushing at her with the Force. "*Tell us now!*"

"It was a bounty hunter called —" The woman twitched, gave one surprised blink, and died. Anakin heard a *whoosh* and looked up in time to see an armored figure wearing a jetpack fly up and around a building. *A bounty hunter! Probably the one who had hired her. And there's no way we can catch him; the speeder is out front, and he'll be gone long before we could get to it.*

Obi-Wan leaned forward. His fingers brushed the assassin's neck; then he held out a small, fat dart about as long as his finger for Anakin's inspection.

"Toxic dart," he said unnecessarily.

And we still don't know who's trying to kill Padmé, Anakin thought. *This is not good.*

CHAPTER 4

Obi-Wan hated making incomplete reports to the Jedi Council, but it was plainly necessary now. First thing next morning, they returned to the Jedi Temple to tell their story to the assembled Council members.

The Jedi Council sat in a circle, to emphasize the equality of the members; nevertheless, everyone knew that Master Yoda and Master Windu were the first among them. When Obi-Wan finished speaking, there was a moment of silence; then everyone looked at Yoda. Yoda studied his fellow Council members briefly, as if he were collecting their votes without speaking. Then he said, "Track down this bounty hunter, you must, Obi-Wan."

"Most importantly, find out who he's working for," Mace Windu added.

Beside him, Obi-Wan felt some of the tension leave Anakin. He appreciated Anakin's confidence in his ability to find the assassin, but Anakin should have learned by this time that receiving an assignment didn't necessarily mean completing it successfully. And there was still Padmé to consider. "What about Senator Amidala?" he asked. "She will still need protection."

"Handle that, your Padawan will," Yoda said.

Obi-Wan looked at Yoda in consternation. Anakin, alone, guarding Padmé . . . *He's too young, and too interested in her. They should assign someone else.* But he couldn't say that to the Jedi Council in front of Anakin, not without a strong reason. All he had was an uncomfortable feeling. He stayed silent.

"Anakin," Mace Windu said, "escort the Senator back to her home planet. She'll be safer there. And don't use registered transport. Travel as refugees."

"It will be very difficult to get Senator Amidala to leave the capital," Anakin said.

At least he's thinking. Obi-Wan began to feel less worried. As long as Anakin thought about what he was doing, instead of charging ahead on impulse, he would be fine.

Master Yoda's ears turned down firmly. "Until caught this killer is, our judgment she must respect."

Anakin still looked doubtful — with reason, Obi-Wan thought. *Senator Amidala isn't going to like taking orders from someone she remembers as a little boy.* Mace Windu looked thoughtfully at the two of them, then said, "Anakin, go to the Senate and ask Chancellor Palpatine to speak with her."

The other Council members nodded. It was a

good idea, Obi-Wan had to admit. If anyone could persuade Padmé to follow the Jedi's advice, Palpatine could. So why did he have such a bad feeling about all this?

Anakin hurried past the Senate and into the huge office building beside it. He had only been to the Chancellor's office a few times before, usually with his Master, but there was no way to go wrong. Palpatine's office occupied the very top of the skyscraper.

When he heard the problem, Chancellor Palpatine nodded in understanding. "I will talk to her," he told Anakin. "Senator Amidala will not refuse an executive order. I know her well enough to assure you of that."

"Thank you, Your Excellency." Anakin replied. He took a last glance out the window — the Chancellor's office had a matchless view of the endless city below, and Anakin had always found it compelling.

Before Anakin could say farewell, Palpatine smiled warmly. "So, my young Padawan, they have finally given you an assignment," he said, and Anakin could sense his interest and approval. "Your patience has paid off."

"Your guidance, more than my patience," Anakin said, but he couldn't help being gratified, as always, by Palpatine's interest. When they had first met on Naboo just after the war, Anakin had only been nine. He hadn't really expected so important a person as the Chancellor to remember him. But Chancellor Palpatine had said then that he would follow Anakin's career with interest, and he had done just that. The Chancellor kep his promises; Anakin couldn't understand why Obi-Wan insisted on doubting him just because he was a politician.

"You don't need guidance, Anakin," the Chancellor said seriously. "In time, you will learn to trust your feelings. Then you will be invincible." He turned to walk to the door with Anakin. "I have said it many times: You are the most gifted Jedi I have ever met."

Anakin felt a shiver of pleasure at the compliment. It meant even more, coming from the Chancellor. *He's not even a Jedi, and he can see I have talent!* "Thank you, your Excellency," he said.

Palpatine smiled, as if he knew how good his praise made Anakin feel. "I see you becoming the greatest of all the Jedi, Anakin. Even more powerful than Master Yoda."

Slightly dazzled by such an impressive vision of his future, Anakin could only mutter his thanks and appreciation once more. But as he left the building, he felt as if he were floating on air.

As soon as the Jedi Council adjourned, Obi-Wan went in search of Master Yoda. He couldn't hurt Anakin by expressing his doubts about the mission in public, but he could certainly ask Yoda for advice privately.

He found Yoda making the circuit of the Jedi Temple halls in a floating chair. He was deep in discussion with Master Windu, who walked beside him. The two looked at Obi-Wan encouragingly. Obi-Wan hesitated only a moment when he saw them both. He'd only planned to talk to Master Yoda, but another point of view might be very useful, and Master Windu was certainly as understanding as Master Yoda.

"I am concerned for my Padawan," Obi-Wan told them. "He is not ready to be given this assignment on his own yet."

Yoda tilted his head, looking up at him slantwise. "The Council is confident in this decision, Obi-Wan."

"The boy has exceptional skills," Master Windu added.

"But he still has much to learn, Master," Obi-wan said. "And his abilities have made him . . . well, arrogant."

To his surprise, Yoda nodded emphatically. "Yes, yes," the little Jedi Master said. "It is a flaw more and more common among Jedi. Too sure of themselves they are. Even the older, more experienced ones."

And Master Yoda is worried about it, Obi-Wan thought. *Or he wouldn't be so emphatic, or call it a common flaw.* He thought back to his first encounters with Anakin. The boy had been much older than normal to begin Jedi training — too old, some had said. But if Anakin had been too old to begin training, Obi-Wan had certainly been very young to take on a Padawan apprentice. *Perhaps there was arrogance on more than one side.* Was it really Anakin he doubted, or was it his own abilities as a teacher?

"Remember, Obi-Wan," Master Windu said. "If the prophecy is true, your apprentice is the only one who can bring the Force back into balance."

"If he follows the right path," Obi-Wan said without thinking. Then he did think, and shivered. Prophecies were tricky things, and the dark side of the Force was growing stronger. Anakin would never choose that path, of course, but —

But what would happen if he did?

Padmé dropped a silk jacket into her carry bag and tucked it into place with exaggerated care. She hated to be driven away from Coruscant after all she had gone through to get back in time for the vote. *Be honest; you just hate running away, period.* But Chancellor Palpatine had been very firm.

She saw Dormé give her a wary, sidelong look, and sighed. She shouldn't be taking her temper out on people who had nothing to do with the problem.

She put a skirt into the bag and glared at the doorway, where Anakin stood talking to Jar Jar Binks, just as if this were normal. *There* was the problem — that overgrown apprentice Jedi who'd talked Chancellor Palpatine into making her leave Coruscant.

Jar Jar caught her glare and looked at her uncertainly. Padmé sighed again. This wasn't his fault, either. From Jar Jar's expression, it was clear that Anakin hadn't fully explained. Well, he couldn't; *he* wasn't the Senator, after all. Forcing a smile, she said to Jar Jar, "I am taking an extended leave of absence. It will be your responsibility to take my place in the Senate. Representative Binks, I know I can count on you."

"Mesa honored to be taken on dissa heavy burden," Jar Jar replied, a little pompously. "Mesa accept this with muy muy humility and da —"

Padmé walked over and gave him a hug, which completely derailed his speech. "You are a good friend, Jar Jar," she said. "But I don't wish to hold you up. I'm sure you have a great deal to do."

"Of course, M'lady," Jar Jar said. As he left, he nodded to Anakin, which only made Padmé feel more cross.

As soon as Jar Jar was gone, Padmé turned to Anakin. "I *do not like* this idea of hiding," she complained.

Anakin raised his hands placatingly. "Don't worry," he told her. "Now that the Council has ordered an investigation, it won't take Master Kenobi long to find that bounty hunter."

As if that was the main problem! Padmé frowned at him. "I haven't worked for an entire year to defeat the Military Creation Act in order not to be here when its fate is decided!"

"Sometimes we have to let go of our pride and do what is requested of us."

He sounds as if he's lecturing a small child! Just because he's gotten so tall . . . "Pride?" She drew herself up in all her Senatorial formality and dignity. "Annie, you're young, and you don't have a very firm grip on politics. I suggest you reserve your opinions for some other time."

She saw the flash of hurt in his expression before he, too, sought refuge in formality. "Sorry, *M'lady*," he said. As he turned away, she heard him murmur, "I was only trying to . . ."

To what? To help? Annie had always tried to help. But now she could feel him withdrawing from her, and somehow she knew that he was doing so only because he thought it was what she wanted. "Annie!" she protested. "No!"

His head came up, and he looked at her for a long moment. He seemed almost more hurt than before. Then he said softly, "Please don't call me that."

"What?" She hadn't insulted him; she had only called him —

"Annie."

Bewildered, Padmé stared at him, her anger forgotten. "But I've always called you that. It's your name, isn't it?"

"My name is Anakin," he said, and she heard an echo in his voice of the nine-year-old boy telling her firmly, *My name is Anakin, and I'm a person.* "When you say Annie it's like I'm still a little boy. And I'm not."

"I'm sorry, Anakin," she said sincerely. Then she grinned and let her gaze travel slowly from his feet up — and up — until her head tilted back so that she could see his face. "It's impossible to deny that you've grown up."

Anakin reddened, and his eyes fell. "Master Obi-Wan manages not to see it," he muttered.

"Mentors have a way of seeing more of our faults than we would like," Padmé said, thinking of her own teachers on Naboo. "It's the only way we grow."

"Don't get me wrong," Anakin said, looking up. "Obi-Wan is a great mentor, as wise as Master Yoda and as powerful as Master Windu. I am truly thankful to be his apprentice. Only . . ." He hesitated, as if he weren't sure he should say what he really wanted to.

Padmé nodded reassuringly, and after a moment Anakin went on, "Although I'm a Padawan learner, in some ways — a lot of ways — I'm ahead of him. I'm ready for the trials, I know I am! He knows it, too.

But he feels I'm too unpredictable." He was almost talking to himself now; the words had the sound of something he'd said inside his head many times. "Other Jedi my age have gone through the trials and made it. I know I started my training late, but he won't let me move on."

"That must be frustrating," Padmé said, trying hard to keep from smiling.

"It's worse," Anakin burst out. "He's overly critical. He never listens! He just doesn't understand. It's not fair!"

Despite herself, Padmé laughed. Anakin looked at her in surprise, and she shook her head. "I'm sorry, but you sounded exactly like that little boy I once knew . . . when he didn't get his way."

"I'm not whining," Anakin insisted. "I'm not!"

Still smiling, Padmé shook her head again. "I didn't say it to hurt you."

"I know," Anakin said softly, and she knew that he did.

"Anakin," she said after a moment's silence, "don't try to grow up too fast."

"I am grown up," he replied. "You said it yourself." He looked down into her eyes.

The intensity of his gaze was disturbing. She couldn't remember the last time someone had looked at her like that — not at Senator Amidala or Queen Amidala or the earnest young legislator, but just at

Padmé. *And he has the deepest eyes . . .* She shook herself. "Please don't look at me like that," she said.

Anakin blinked. "Why not?"

"Because I can see what you're thinking." She hadn't meant to say that, straight out.

"Ahh," Anakin nodded, laughing. "So you have Jedi powers, too?"

Padmé turned away. This ex-slave boy had no business laughing at her. "It makes me feel uncomfortable," she said stiffly.

"Sorry, M'lady." Anakin sounded sincere, but Padmé couldn't shake the feeling that he was still laughing at her. Her lips tightened, and she walked firmly away to finish packing.

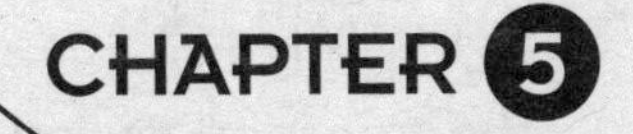

CHAPTER 5

Obi-Wan, Captain Typho, and Dormé all went along with Anakin and Padmé to the spaceport freighter docks. Privately, Obi-Wan felt that even that was too many people, but Captain Typho was Padmé's official security head, and Padmé was worried about her handmaiden, who would be taking her place as "Senator Amidala" in hopes of fooling the assassins, so he hadn't tried very hard to talk them out of coming. He had, however, insisted that no one but Padmé and Anakin would get off the little transport that carried them to the docks. A Jedi, a Naboo officer in uniform, and "Senator Amidala" would attract far too much attention, and the whole point of sending Padmé by ordinary freighter was to get her away from Coruscant unnoticed.

Anakin and Padmé wore loose peasant clothes of gray and brown. Anakin had bundled his Padawan braid into a knot at the back of his head to make it less obvious. A Jedi Padawan accompanying a young woman on a refugee transport would be unusual enough to cause considerable comment. For the hundredth time, Obi-Wan studied them, and decided again that their disguises would do.

The transport pulled up at the docks at last. While Padmé and Dormé began a rather tearful good-bye, Obi-Wan pulled Anakin aside. Ignoring Anakin's frown, he repeated the mission instructions, with a little added emphasis. "Anakin, you stay on Naboo. Don't do anything without first consulting either myself or the Council."

"Yes, Master," Anakin said in the tones of someone who'd heard this too many times already.

Obi-Wan sighed, wishing he could believe it. Not that he thought Anakin was lying; he was quite sure his apprentice *meant* to follow instructions. Anakin always meant well. But Anakin was impulsive, and too sure of himself and his abilities. If he thought there was a need, he might easily forget his promise and jeopardize everything. *This is the only way to be sure of Padmé's safety,* Obi-Wan told himself. That last assassin had come too close. Still, he could not shake his feeling of unease.

Padmé finished saying farewell to her handmaiden, and joined them. Her expression was grave. Obi-Wan nodded and said, "I will get to the bottom of this plot quickly, M'lady. You'll be back here in no time."

"I will be most grateful for your speed, Master Jedi," Padmé replied formally.

She's still angry about leaving Coruscant, Obi-Wan thought. He was almost ready to call the trip off, to look for some other alternative, but Anakin picked up their battered travel cases and said, "Time to go."

Padmé gave Dormé one last hug, and she and Anakin went to the door of the transport, where R2-D2 waited to accompany them.

"May the Force be with you," Obi-Wan said to Anakin.

"May the Force be with you, Master," Anakin replied.

Why do I feel as if we're saying good-bye to each other for the last time? Obi-Wan shook himself. He was doing just what he always scolded Anakin for — focusing on the negative. But as he watched Anakin and Padmé and R2 disappear into the spaceport, he could not help murmuring to Captain Typho, "I hope he doesn't try anything foolish."

Captain Typho glanced at Obi-Wan and shook his head. "I'd be more concerned about her doing something than him."

Well, you don't know Anakin. On the other hand, some of the things Padmé had done during the Naboo war had been just as risky as anything his apprentice had come up with. Perhaps that was the source of his unease.

They waited in silence until the freighter took off. Obi-Wan even stretched his Jedi abilities to make sure that Anakin and Padmé were on board — he'd almost been afraid that Padmé would talk Anakin into letting her stay at the last minute.

As soon as he knew that everything had gone smoothly, Obi-Wan sent the transport back toward the diplomatic section of Coruscant. He let Captain Typho and Dormé off at the Senator's apartment to continue their dangerous masquerade, and went on to the Jedi Temple. He had promised Padmé he'd finish this investigation quickly, and he wanted to get to work.

The analysis cubicles at the Temple were busy, but he found an empty one. Pulling out the toxic dart that had killed the attempted assassin, he put it on the sensor tray. "I need to know where this came from and who made it," he told the Analysis Droid.

"One moment, please," said the droid. It retracted the tray and began its work.

Obi-Wan waited, watching diagrams and data scroll rapidly past on the droid's display. Then, to his surprise, the screen went blank.

"Markings cannot be identified," the droid announced. "As you can see on your screen, subject weapon does not exist in any known culture. Probably self-made by a warrior not associated with any known society. Stand away from the sensor tray, please." The tray slid out, waiting for him to take back the dart.

"Excuse me," Obi-Wan said. "Could you try again, please?"

"Master Jedi, our records are very thorough," the droid said. If it were human, Obi-Wan thought it would have sounded miffed at the suggestion that it hadn't checked everything the first time. "If I can't tell you where it came from, nobody can."

Obi-Wan looked at the dart. *Nobody can? Hmm. I wonder . . .* "Thank you for your assistance," he told the droid as he pocketed the dart. He turned away and said, half to himself, "I know who can identify this."

He could have sworn he heard an incredulous sniff from behind him as he left the analysis cubicle.

At first glance, Dex's Diner looked like every other low-level eatery in this tough part of town. Shiny maroon booths lined the walls, slick tile covered the floor, and the counter along the wall was edged in shiny chrome. Dex's was, however, much cleaner and smelled far better than most of the other such places Obi-Wan had been in.

The Waitress Droid cleaning the booths was initially unhelpful when he asked to see Dexter. "He's not in trouble," Obi-Wan told her. "It's personal."

The droid gave him a long, evaluating look. Then

she called through the open serving hatch, "Someone to see you, honey." Lowering her voice slightly, she added, "A Jedi, by the looks of him."

A cloud of steam and a huge head poked out of the serving hatch. "Obi-Wan!" Dexter called cheerfully. "Take a seat! I'll be right with you!"

Smiling slightly, Obi-Wan chose an empty booth. The Waitress Droid, reassured at last, brought over two mugs of steaming ardees. A moment later, Dexter emerged from the back room. He hadn't changed much since the last time Obi-Wan had seen him — he was a little older, a little balder, and perhaps a little heavier, though with his bulk a few more pounds made almost no difference. Beaming, he squeezed his bulk and his four arms into the seat across from Obi-Wan.

"So, my friend, what can I do for you?" he asked, gesturing with all four arms.

"You can tell me what this is," Obi-Wan said, sliding the dart across the table.

Dexter's eyes widened. "Well, whaddya know," he said softly. With a delicacy surprising in one so large, he picked up the dart and turned it over. "I ain't seen one of these since I was prospecting on Subterrel, beyond the Outer Rim."

"Do you know where it came from?" Obi-Wan asked, leaning forward.

Dexter grinned. "This baby belongs to them cloners. What you got here is a Kamino Saberdart."

So much for "If I can't tell you, nobody can," Obi-Wan thought with considerable satisfaction. "A Kamino Saberdart?" he repeated. "I wonder why it didn't show up in our analysis archive."

"It's these funny little cuts on the side that give it away," Dexter said, pointing. "Those Analysis Droids you've got over there only focus on symbols, you know." He grinned again, hugely pleased, and added slyly, "I should think you Jedi would have more respect for the difference between knowledge and wisdom."

"Well, Dex, if droids could think, we wouldn't be here, would we?" Obi-Wan said, and they both laughed. Obi-Wan looked at the dart again, and sobered. "Kamino," he said thoughtfully. "Doesn't sound familiar. Is it part of the Republic?"

"No, it's beyond the Outer Rim," Dexter told him. "About twelve parsecs outside the Rishi Maze, toward the south. It should be easy to find, even for those droids in your archive." He paused briefly; when Obi-Wan didn't react, he went on, "These Kaminoans keep to themselves. They're cloners. Damned good ones, too."

Obi-Wan looked at Dexter, considering. "Cloners? Are they friendly?"

"It depends," Dexter replied seriously.

"On what, Dex?"

This time, Dex's grin had very little humor in it. "On how good your manners are . . . and how big your pocketbook is."

* * *

The hold of the freighter was dark and crowded; nothing at all like the light, airy spaces of the royal Naboo cruiser. *This is what star travel is like for most people*, Padmé told herself. It reminded her a little of her work with the relief group on Shadda-Bi-Boran when she was eight. She hadn't thought about that in years.

Giving herself a shake, she studied the faces around her. Some seemed tired and worn; some seemed bursting with new hope. None of them looked like a possible assassin. *But what does an assassin look like? I've never seen one. Just that droid at my window last night. Maybe assassins look just like anyone else.* She shivered, wondering what kind of person would hunt and kill other intelligent beings for a living.

Beside her, Anakin shifted in his sleep once again. He had been tossing and turning ever since he lay down. Padmé was just wondering whether this was normal for him, when she heard him mutter, "No," and then, "No! Mom, no!" She leaned toward him and saw that he was sweating. Gently, she laid a hand on his arm, hoping she wouldn't have to shake him awake.

Anakin was apparently a light sleeper. His eyes opened, and he looked at her in evident confusion. "What?"

"You seemed to be having a nightmare," Padmé told him.

Anakin gave her a penetrating look. Padmé looked away and saw R2-D2 rolling up, carrying two chunks of bread. As she blinked in mild surprise, the little droid extended a tube and filled two bowls with mush. *I thought this ship didn't serve droids. Well, I always knew R2 was resourceful.* "Are you hungry?" she asked Anakin.

He nodded, and she passed him one of the bowls. "Thanks," he said.

"We went to lightspeed a while ago," Padmé said neutrally. If he didn't want to talk about his nightmare, she wouldn't force him to.

"I look forward to seeing Naboo again. I've thought about it every day since I left. It's by far the most beautiful place I've ever seen." He gave her an intense look as he spoke, as if willing her to understand some secret meaning in his words.

Padmé shifted uncomfortably. She didn't want him to mean more than what he said. She certainly didn't want him idealizing Naboo and . . . and its people. He would surely be disappointed. "It may not be as you remember it," she said. "Time changes perception."

"Sometimes it does," Anakin said, still with that same intense gaze. "Sometimes for the better."

More uncomfortable than ever, Padmé looked down and took a mouthful of mush. *Time to change the subject,* she thought. "It must be difficult having sworn your life to the Jedi," she said. "Not being able to visit the places you like, or do the things you like . . ." Too late, she remembered that Anakin had been a slave when they met, even less in control of his life than a Jedi apprentice. To him, being a Jedi must mean more freedom in his life, not less.

But Anakin was nodding. "Or be with the people I love," he said.

"Are you allowed to love?" Padmé asked. "I thought it was forbidden for a Jedi."

"Attachment is forbidden," Anakin said slowly. "Possession is forbidden. But compassion, which I would define as unconditional love, is central to a Jedi's life. So you might say we're encouraged to love."

Was this thoughtful, serious young man the same Anakin as the little boy she remembered? "You have changed so much," she said without thinking.

"You haven't changed a bit," Anakin told her. "You're exactly the way I remember you in my dreams. I doubt if Naboo has changed much, either."

He dreams about me? She wasn't sure whether that pleased her or frightened her. "It hasn't," she admitted, and then firmly turned the subject. "You were dreaming about your mother earlier, weren't you?"

Anakin looked away. "Yes. I left Tatooine so long ago, my memory of her is fading. I don't want to lose it. And lately I've been seeing her in my dreams —

vivid dreams. Scary dreams." His voice became lower and softer. "I worry about her."

No wonder he would rather dream about me . . . and Naboo, of course. Padmé looked at him in sudden sympathy. He ducked his head to continue eating. *He's more worried than he wants to admit. And he's a Jedi; they just* know *things sometimes.* A shiver of apprehension ran through her as she remembered the strong, gentle woman she had met so long ago on Tatooine. She wanted to believe that nothing awful could have happened to her, but Shmi Skywalker had been a slave, like her son, and Tatooine had so many dangers. . . .

CHAPTER 6

The Jedi archives had always been one of Obi-Wan's favorite places in the Jedi Temple, at once peaceful and busy. The silent banks of computer panels held more information than any other data center in the galaxy, and no matter what the time of day or night, three or four consoles were always occupied by Jedi studying trends or searching for some key piece of knowledge that would aid them on their missions. Today, not only were several consoles occupied, but four or five Jedi sat scattered around various tables in the center of the room, studying printed materials from the archives. Even with all the information the Storage Droids had put into the computers, some things still needed to be looked at in their original forms.

It should have been simple to get the coordinates for Kamino from the computers, but to Obi-Wan's surprise, there were no records of the place. After spending half an hour fruitlessly searching the information banks, Obi-Wan pressed a button that would summon one of the archivists to help him. Then he stood up, stretched, and began to pace, careful not to disturb his fellow Jedi at their work.

Near the doorway, Obi-Wan stopped by a row of bronze busts. He realized after a moment that the bust directly in front of him was Count Dooku, and he studied it with interest. There was nothing in the long, chiseled face and stern expression to hint at the path he had chosen. Leader of the Separatists, who might well plunge the Republic into civil war — how could a Jedi, even one who had left the order, come to that? And why *had* he left? It had happened shortly after the Naboo war. Obi-Wan had been off-planet and busy with his new responsibilities as a full-fledged Jedi Knight; by the time he came back to Coruscant, the Count was gone. He had never found out what happened.

He heard a small sound, and turned to find the Jedi archivist, Jocasta Nu, standing next to him. With her neat gray hair and thin face, she looked deceptively frail in her Jedi robes; most people would never guess that she was more than a desk-bound librarian. Obi-Wan knew better. Jocasta had been a formidable Jedi warrior in her youth, and though she now spent most of her time organizing and searching the archives for her fellow Jedi, she still went out on missions from time to time. "Did you call for assistance?" she asked pointedly.

"Yes," Obi-Wan said, tearing his eyes away from the bust. "Yes, I did."

Jocasta smiled in understanding. "He has a powerful face, doesn't he? He was one of the most brilliant Jedi I have had the privilege of knowing."

"I never understood why he quit," Obi-Wan said. Jocasta Nu was also a Jedi; surely she had wondered the same things he did. "Only twenty Jedi have ever left the Order."

"The Lost Twenty," the archivist said with a sigh. "And Count Dooku was the most recent — and the most painful." She paused. "No one likes to talk about it. His leaving was a great loss."

If nobody wanted to talk about it, there was only one way to find out. "What happened?" Obi-Wan asked bluntly.

Jocasta smiled slightly, but answered readily enough. "Well, Count Dooku was always a bit out of step with the decisions of the Council." She gave Obi-Wan a look that he could not decipher. "Much like your old Master, Qui-Gon Jinn."

"Really?" The idea was surprising . . . and disturbing. *But Master Qui-Gon would never have left the Order. Never.*

"Oh, yes," the elder Jedi said. "They were alike in many ways. Very individual thinkers. Idealists . . ."

She looked at the bust and went on, half to herself, "He was always striving to become a more powerful Jedi. He wanted to be the best. With a lightsaber, in the old style of fencing, he had no match. His knowledge of the Force was . . . unique."

He sounds a little like Anakin, Obi-Wan thought, and frowned.

Jocasta sighed and turned her head, as if she could not bear to look at the bust any longer. "In the end, I think he left because he lost faith in the Republic. He always had very high expectations of government. He disappeared for nine or ten years, then just showed up recently as the head of the Separatist movement."

Obi-Wan waited, but she didn't seem inclined to say any more. "Interesting," he said at last. "I'm still not sure I understand completely."

"Well, I'm sure you didn't call me over here for a history lesson," the archivist said. "Are you having a problem, Master Kenobi?"

Obi-Wan gestured at the screen he had been using. "Yes, I'm trying to find a planet system called Kamino. It doesn't seem to show up on any of the archive charts."

"Kamino?" Jocasta repeated. "It's not a system I'm familiar with. Let me see." She studied the screen for a moment. "Are you sure you have the right coordinates?"

"According to my information, it should be in this quadrant somewhere — just south of the Rishi Maze."

"No coordinates?" The archivist frowned. "It sounds like the sort of directions you'd get from a street tout — some old miner or Furbog trader."

"All three, actually," Obi-Wan said with a smile, thinking of Dex.

Jocasta gave him a skeptical look. "Are you sure it exists?"

"Absolutely."

She looked at him a moment longer, then nodded. "Let me do a gravitational scan." Her fingers flew over the controls, and the screen display changed. She studied it for a moment, and pointed. "There are some inconsistencies here. Maybe the planet you're seeking was destroyed."

That was possible, but — "Wouldn't that be on record?"

"It ought to be," the archivist admitted. "Unless it was very recent." She looked at him and shook her head. "I hate to say it, but it looks like the system you're searching for doesn't exist."

Obi-Wan thought of the toxic dart in his pocket. "That's impossible. Perhaps the archives are incomplete."

Jocasta stiffened, as if he had insulted her personally. "The archives are comprehensive and totally secure, my young Jedi," she snapped. "One thing you may be absolutely sure of — if an item does not appear in our records, it does not exist!"

This was starting to sound familiar — *If I can't tell you where it came from, nobody can . . .. If it isn't in our records, it does not exist . . .* Obi-Wan stared at the map screen and frowned suddenly. Gravitational anomalies . . . *something* had been where Dexter said the Kamino system was, records or not.

Obi-Wan shook his head. None of this made sense. According to the Jedi records, Padmé's attempted assassin had been killed by an unidentified dart from a nonexistent world. He didn't know which was more disturbing — reaching a dead end in his investigation or finding such obvious gaps in the Jedi information systems. And he had run out of other sources.

He thanked the archivist for her help, and copied the map to a portable display reader, to think about later. He must know *someone* who could think of another place to try.

Naboo looked and sounded and smelled even better than Anakin's memories of it. The rose-gold domes of the city, the flowers that scented the air, the distant music of the waterfalls — nothing had changed. Well, this time there were no armies of Trade Federation Battle Droids trying to kill them, but that could only be counted a plus. Except for the cold, it was perfect.

Padmé seemed to enjoy being back on Naboo as much as he did. She insisted that they go straight from the spaceport to the palace, so that she could report to the Queen, but once that was settled, she seemed to shed some of her fierce, determined Senatorial persona. She seemed more like the Padmé Anakin had known on Tatooine when he was small. The thought made Anakin wonder about Padmé's girlhood, and he asked, "Tell me, did you dream of power and politics when you were a little girl?"

Padmé laughed, startled, and turned to look at him. "No, that was the last thing I thought of." Her face took on a thoughtful, remembering look. "I was elected for the most part because of my conviction that reform was possible. I wasn't the youngest Queen ever elected, but now that I think back on it, I'm not sure I was old enough." She glanced back toward the palace, and her eyes lingered on a section of the polished surface that was newer than the rest, shaped like a blaster scar that had been repaired. "I'm not sure I was ready," she murmured.

"The people you served thought you did a good job," Anakin pointed out, hoping to cheer her up. "I heard they tried to amend the Constitution so you could stay in office."

"Popular rule is not democracy, Annie," Padmé said. "It gives the people what they want, not what they need. Truthfully, I was relieved when my two terms were up — but when the Queen asked me to serve as Senator, I couldn't refuse her."

"I think the Republic needs you," Anakin said firmly as they reached the palace steps. "I'm glad you chose to serve."

Padmé smiled at him, and they went inside. An aide conducted them up the stairs to the marble-lined throne room. It was odd to see Queen Jamillia on the throne, wearing the royal face paint, when in Anakin's memory it was Padmé who belonged there. But the handmaidens in their flame-red robes were the same, and so were some of the Queen's advisors. Anakin even recognized one of them, Sio Bibble, who had stayed on Naboo during the war.

The Queen greeted Padmé like an old friend. "We've been worried about you," she said, taking Padmé's hand. "I'm so glad you are safe."

"Thank you, Your Highness," Padmé replied. "I only wish I could have served you better by staying on Coruscant for the vote."

"Given the circumstances, Senator, it was the only decision Her Highness could have made," Sio Bibble said sternly.

"How many systems have joined Count Dooku and the Separatists?" the Queen asked.

"Thousands," Padmé said. "And more are leaving the Republic every day. If the Senate votes to create an army, I'm sure it's going to push us into a civil war."

Anakin let his attention drift as the two women discussed the possibility of war, the reactions of the bureaucrats, and the position the Trade Federation would take in any conflict. He never had understood what Padmé found so interesting about politics. His attention came back to the conversation with a snap when he heard Padmé say, "There are rumors, Your Highness, that the Trade Federation Army was not reduced as they were ordered."

The Queen looked startled and skeptical. Anakin didn't blame her; after what they had done on Naboo, it was unthinkable for the Trade Federation to keep their huge armies of Battle Droids. But Anakin suspected that Padmé was right, and he wondered why the Jedi had not investigated the rumors. He remembered the Naboo war all too well, and it galled him to think that the Trade Federation had weaseled out of its well-deserved punishment.

"We must keep our faith in the Republic," Queen Jamillia said firmly. "The day we stop believing democracy can work is the day we lose it."

"Let us pray that day never comes," Padmé murmured.

"In the meantime, we must consider your own safety," the Queen went on. Anakin stiffened, wondering whether she intended to discuss arrangements in front of all her attendants, but Sio Bibble nodded and the rest of the court melted away. When only he and the Queen were left, he looked at Anakin and said, "What is your suggestion, Master Jedi?"

Anakin opened his mouth but Padmé was there before him. "Anakin's not a Jedi yet, Counselor. He's still a Padawan learner. I was thinking —"

"Hey, hold on a minute," Anakin said, thinking, *A Padawan is still a member of the Order, and this is my assignment!* Besides, she hadn't had to make a point of it. His Padawan braid was clearly visible; Sio Bibble must have seen it and known what it meant.

"Excuse me!" Padmé said stiffly over her shoulder. Turning back to the Queen, she went on, "I was thinking I would stay in the Lake Country. There are some places up there that are very isolated."

She has no business dismissing me like that! Anakin thought angrily. "Excuse *me,*" he said coldly. "I am in charge of security here, M'lady."

Padmé turned and said deliberately, "Annie, my life is at risk, and this is my home. I know it very well; that is why we're here. I think it would be wise for you to take advantage of my knowledge in this instance."

That's not the problem, and you know it! Anakin almost blurted out the words, but he saw the Queen and Sio Bibble exchange amused glances, and restrained himself. Padmé was trying to annoy him; she had called him Annie again, the little-boy name he was growing to hate. But he couldn't take chances with her safety just because he was annoyed with her. Taking a deep breath, he muttered, "Sorry, M'lady."

"Perfect," the Queen said. "It's settled, then." She rose, and looked at Padmé. "I had an audience with your father yesterday. He hopes you will visit your mother before you leave. Your family is very worried."

That was unexpected, but it didn't sound like a security problem. And Padmé's family — Anakin had never thought about what sort of family she must have. He looked at her, and was surprised to see a faintly apprehensive look on her face. What was she worried about? Maybe she was afraid they'd tell him about her childhood pranks. He grinned suddenly. It would be nice to have some ammunition to use the next time Padmé started calling him Annie. Still grinning, he followed her out of the throne room.

Yoda looked out over the training floor, watching the class of four-year-olds at their practice. The Force was bright and strong in these children of all species, and it was a pleasure to teach them. Each child held a miniature, low-powered lightsaber and wore a training helmet that could block out sight, so that they had to depend on the Force in order to strike the small droids that danced around them. The intense focus of so many young minds made Yoda almost forget his own centuries of age.

"Don't think," he said, sensing a faltering in one small figure. "Feel. Be as one with the Force. Help you, it will."

The child relaxed, and her next swing connected with the training remote. Yoda smiled. Then he saw a different movement on the far side of the room. Obi-Wan Kenobi came through the door, and though he smiled at the practicing children, Yoda sensed that his mind was elsewhere. "Younglings, enough," Yoda called. "A visitor we have. Welcome him."

As the children powered down their lightsabers, Yoda moved slowly forward. "Master Obi-Wan Kenobi, meet the mighty Bear Clan," he said, nodding at the children.

"Welcome, Master Obi-Wan!" the children chorused.

Obi-Wan nodded a greeting, but turned at once to Yoda. "I am sorry to disturb you, Master," he said.

"What help to you can I be?" Yoda answered.

"I'm looking for a planet described to me by an old friend. I trust him. But the system doesn't show up on the archive maps."

The implications were obvious, and serious, but there was no reason to upset the children. And this would make an excellent training problem. Yoda twitched his ears up and said calmly, "Lost a planet, Master Obi-Wan has. How embarrassing." One of the children smothered a giggle; he pretended not to notice. "Liam, the shades. An interesting puzzle." He stumped over to Obi-Wan and waved his cane at his class. "Gather, younglings, around the map reader. Clear your minds, and find Obi-Wan's wayward planet, we will try. Bobby, the lights, please."

Obediently, the children clustered around the shaft of the map reader as the lights dimmed. This class had not seen it in use before, and there were exclamations of surprise when Obi-Wan brought out a small glass ball — the portable map record — and placed it in the hollow top of the reader shaft. The surprise turned to delighted laughs when a three-dimensional hologram of the galaxy sprang up, occupying a large part of the room. Stars of varying brightness seemed to float in the classroom air, and a few of the children tried to catch them.

Obi-Wan walked into the hologram and stopped. "This is where it ought to be — but it isn't. Gravity is pulling all the stars in this area inward to this spot. There should be a star here . . . but there isn't."

"Most interesting," Yoda said. "Gravity's silhouette remains, but the star and all of its planets have disappeared. How can this be?" Again, he turned to his class. "Now, younglings, in your mind, what is the first thing you see? An answer? A thought? Anyone?"

There was a moment of silence. Then a boy raised his hand. Yoda nodded, and the child said, "Master? Because someone erased it from the archive memory."

"Yes!" called the other children happily. "That's what happened. Someone erased it!"

Obi-Wan was staring at the children. A small, serious girl looked at him and explained, "If the planet blew up, the gravity would go away."

Yoda chuckled, as much at the expression on Obi-Wan's face as out of pleasure at the performance of his students. "Truly wonderful, the mind of a child is. The Padawan is right. Go to the center of gravity's pull, and find your planet you will."

Still looking a little stunned, Obi-Wan retrieved his map. "But Master Yoda," he asked as he turned to go, "who could have erased information from the archives? That's impossible. Isn't it?"

Strong is the Force with this one. He sees past his own troubles. Yoda frowned, but he could not refuse an answer to one who had asked the proper question. "Dangerous and disturbing this puzzle is," he admitted. "Only a Jedi could have erased those files." He felt Obi-Wan's startled concern, and nodded. "Who, and why, harder to answer are. Meditate on this, I will. May the Force be with you."

Obi-Wan repeated the wish with more sincerity in his voice than was usual, even among Jedi. As he walked back to his class, Yoda found himself nodding. *May the Force be with us all.*

CHAPTER 7

Obi-Wan gave his starfighter a last inspection. The R4 droid swiveled in its socket in the wing of the small red-and-white spacecraft, and everything seemed to be in order.

Beside him, Master Windu watched, his dark face solemn. "Be wary," he said as Obi-Wan finished. "This disturbance in the Force is growing stronger."

Obi-Wan nodded. Every Jedi could feel it now, and he'd heard that even some of the students could sense it.

More than ever, it made him worry about Anakin and Padmé. *I don't care how sure the Council is; we should not have been given this assignment. He's drawn to her too strongly.* Master Windu looked at him, as if asking what was wrong. Obi-Wan sighed. "I'm afraid Anakin won't be able to protect the Senator," he said.

Mace Windu considered. "Why?" he asked calmly.

"He has a — an emotional connection with her," Obi-Wan said. "It's been there since he was a boy. Now he is confused, distracted —"

"Obi-Wan, you must have faith that he will take the right path," Master Windu interrupted.

Obi-Wan nodded. Yet he could not help wondering whether Master Windu really understood what he was trying to say. Perhaps he should leave a message for Master Yoda. No, Master Windu would surely tell him, and in any case, there was nothing any of them could do about it now. *Anakin will have to manage on his own.* He climbed into the starfighter and punched the button to close the canopy.

"May the Force be with you," Mace Windu said as the protective cover slid closed.

The planet Kamino was exactly where it ought to have been. Obi-Wan frowned and muttered to R4 as he brought his starfighter in toward the planet. In spite of Master Yoda's words, he hadn't wanted to admit to himself that someone had tampered with the Jedi archives, but plainly, someone had. *Who? And what else have they erased?* He shook his head and put the questions out of his mind. That was Master Yoda's problem now. His job was to track down the mysterious bounty hunter in the silver armor and jetpack.

His request for landing instructions was answered

by a Kaminoan who introduced herself as Taun We. "You'll want to land at Tipoca City," she told him. "There's an open landing platform on the south side; I'll transmit the coordinates."

Obi-Wan took his time about landing. Kamino's sun was a hot star, and most of its surface was water; the combination meant that clouds and rain wrapped the planet almost continuously. *Good weather here probably means a day when there's no lightning and the wind isn't blowing the rain sideways,* Obi-Wan thought as he wrestled with his controls. When the ship was down at last, he donned his cloak and ran through the dark, driving rain toward the tower at the far side of the landing platform. As he neared, a door slid open. Gratefully, he went inside.

The sounds of the storm outside cut off abruptly as the door slid shut behind him. The inner walls of the tower glowed bright white, lighting the hall with cool, shadowless brilliance. The sudden light made Obi-Wan squint, unable to see clearly for a moment.

"Master Jedi, so good to see you," said a soft voice.

Obi-Wan pushed back his soaking hood, wiped the rain from his face, and saw Taun We waiting for him. Their brief discussion over the viewscreen had shown him her huge almond-shaped eyes and paper-white skin, but he had not realized how tall and thin she was. More surprising was the genuine pleasure he sensed in her as she went on, "The Prime Minister expects you."

"I'm expected?" Had someone warned these people about him? Why?

"Of course!" she replied cheerfully. "He is anxious to see you. After all these years, we were beginning to think you weren't coming. Now please, this way!"

This is extremely odd, Obi-Wan thought as they made their way through the corridors of the city. But he sensed no fear or dismay, not from his guide and not from any of the other beings they passed. The Kaminoan took him through a maze of corridors directly to a large office. The room had no windows, but it hardly needed any; its walls glowed with the same cool, bright light as the corridors. As they entered, another Kaminoan rose politely from his seat behind a wide glass-and-metal desk. Taun We introduced him as Lama Su, the Prime Minister.

"I trust you are going to enjoy your stay," Lama Su told him once the courtesies were out of the way. "We are most happy you have arrived at the best part of the season."

They call this good weather? But remembering Dexter's comment about manners, Obi-Wan smiled and nodded. "You make me feel most welcome."

"You will be delighted to hear that we are on schedule," Lama Su continued. "Two hundred thousand units are ready, with another million well on the way."

Two hundred thousand . . . units? Of what? "That is . . . good news," Obi-Wan said cautiously.

"Please tell your Master Sifo-Dyas that we have every confidence his order will be met on time and in full. He is well, I hope?"

Obi-Wan blinked. "I'm sorry — Master . . . ?"

"Jedi Master Sifo-Dyas." Lama Su tilted his head forward. "He's still a leading member of the Jedi Council, is he not?"

"I'm afraid Master Sifo-Dyas was killed almost ten years ago," Obi-Wan said slowly. *More like eleven or twelve years, I think — but I could have the times mixed up. I'll have to check with Master Yoda later.*

"I'm sorry to hear that." Lama Su sounded sincere, and Obi-Wan sensed no falsehood in his statement. "But I'm sure he would have been proud of the army we've built for him."

An army? Dexter had said the Kaminoans were cloners. *A million units,* Obi-Wan thought numbly. *An army of a million troops. That's enough to conquer the Republic.* He swallowed hard, then hesitated, trying to think how best to phrase his next question. "Tell me, Prime Minister," he said at last, "when my Master first contacted you about the army, did he say who it was for?"

"Of course he did," Lama Su said in a reassuring tone. "This army is for the Republic."

For the Republic? Obi-Wan struggled to make sense of what he was being told. Sifo-Dyas had ordered this army ten years ago — that must have been just after the Naboo war. He had been a powerful Jedi. Had he forseen the need, even then?

Lama Su rose and went on, "You must be anxious to inspect the units for yourself."

He has no idea how true that is, Obi-Wan thought. Aloud, he said, "That's why I'm here."

After a brief visit with Padmé's family, Anakin escorted her up to the Lake Country. The lodge Padmé had chosen for them to stay at was beautiful, like everything else on Naboo, and just as isolated as she had promised. The island it stood on was one of several that glowed a rich green in the middle of a shimmering blue lake at the foot of a mountain range. The caretaker drove them out to the lodge in a water speeder, which gave Anakin plenty of time to study it. It only took a few seconds to see that anyone approaching the lodge would be easy to spot long before they arrived, so Anakin relaxed and enjoyed the view.

The lodge itself seemed large to Anakin, though it was small compared to the palaces that lined the streets of the capital. He paused on a terrace just outside, leaning on a carved marble balustrade that separated the terrace from the flower garden just below. Padmé joined him, and it was no effort at all to turn his attention from the distant mountains to the girl beside him.

"I love the water," Padmé said dreamily.

"I do, too," Anakin said, looking down at her. "I guess it comes from growing up on a desert planet."

Padmé gave him a sidelong look, then dropped her eyes to the lake once more. "We used to lie on the sand and let the sun dry us, and try to guess the names of the birds singing."

"I don't like sand. It's coarse and rough and irritating, and it gets everywhere. Not like here. Here everything is soft . . . and smooth." Without thinking, he touched her arm.

Padmé gave him another nervous glance and waved at the lake, pulling her arm away as if by accident. "There was a very old man who lived on the island," she said. "He used to make glass out of sand. And vases and necklaces out of the glass." She smiled, and looked up at him as if to share her memories. "They were magical."

"Everything here is magical," Anakin said, staring down into her eyes. She had the most beautiful brown eyes. . . .

"You could look into the glass and see the water. The way it ripples and moves," Padmé went on. She lowered her eyes. "It looked so real . . . but it wasn't."

"Sometimes, when you believe something to be real, it becomes real."

"I used to think that if you looked too deeply into the glass you would lose yourself," Padmé said softly.

But she didn't seem to be talking about the glass anymore.

"I think it's true," Anakin said. He felt warm, and he couldn't look away from Padmé. He didn't *want* to look away. He wanted to be here, with her, forever. He bent forward and kissed her.

At first, she didn't resist; then suddenly she pulled away. The abrupt movement brought Anakin back to his senses as well, and he let her go.

"No. I shouldn't have done that," Padmé said.

"I'm sorry," Anakin replied. Well, he wasn't sorry that he had kissed her; his lips still tingled from the pressure of hers. But he was sorry that she was distressed. "When I'm around you, my mind is no longer my own."

"It's the situation," Padmé said, carefully not looking at him. "The stress —"

"The view," Anakin put in softly, his eyes lingering on the soft curve of her neck. But Padmé's head was still turned away, and she didn't see.

Lama Su and Taun We began Obi-Wan's tour with the replication area where racks of embryos were growing in fluid-filled glass balls. "Very impressive," Obi-Wan said.

"I'd hoped you would be pleased," Lama Su said, smiling. "Clones *can* think creatively. You'll find that they are immensely superior to droids."

You may be manufacturing them, but they're people,

not droids. Obi-Wan could feel the living Force in each of the clones, just as it existed in every other living thing. But he kept his face calm as they went on to an ordinary classroom filled with boys about ten years old. Except that these boys had identical faces below the exact same black, curly hair.

"You mentioned growth acceleration," Obi-Wan said in a neutral tone.

"Oh, yes," Lama Su said earnestly. "It's essential. Otherwise, a mature clone would take a lifetime to grow. Now we can do it in half the time."

Obi-Wan stared at the boys. "These?"

"Were started about five years ago," Lama Su replied, obviously pleased by Obi-Wan's surprise.

Their next stop was an eating area. Hundreds of identical young men sat at long tables. Again, Obi-Wan saw the same dark hair, the same strong features. Even their expressions were the same.

"You'll find they are totally obedient, taking any order without question," Lama Su said. "We modified their genetic structure to make them less independent than the original host."

"Who *was* the original host?" Obi-Wan asked, hoping the question sounded casual.

"A bounty hunter called Jango Fett," Lama Su answered readily. "We felt a Jedi would be the perfect choice, but Sifo-Dyas handpicked Jango Fett himself."

Anakin, Obi-Wan, and Padmé meet again after many years.

Padmé discusses the identity of her attackers with Mace Windu

Zam Wesell takes aim.

Obi-Wan scouts out the scene at the Outlander club.

The Jedi Masters ponder their next move.

Anakin feels ready for his first solo mission.

Master Yoda's young
pupils hold some very
important answers.

A view of the Jedi Temple Archive Library.

Yoda ponders the signs of the past, present, and future.

Obi-Wan and Taun We interrupt the Fetts at home.

A Jedi and a Senator in disguise,
accompanied by a very familiar droid.

Jango Fett and Obi-Wan face off on the ground . . .

. . . until Jango takes to the air!

Slave I vs. the Delta-7 Jedi starfighter.

Boba Fett: born to be a bounty hunter.

Watto learns that his former slave has become a Jedi.

Anakin enters the lives of Beru Whitesun and Owen Lars.

A love that cannot be denied.

A secret factory produces deadly clone troopers.

The Senate: cradle of galactic democracy.

Jar Jar addresses the Senate.

“I will create a grand army of the Republic to counter the increasing threats of the Separatists.” —Chancellor Palpatine

or battle.

"You have unusual powers, young Padawan.
But not enough to save you this time."—Count Dooku

"Powerful you have become, Dooku.
The dark side I sense in you." —Yoda

A bounty hunter! Obi-Wan kept his expression neutral. "Where is this bounty hunter now?"

"He lives here, but he's free to come and go as he pleases," Lama Su replied. He waved Obi-Wan through into the sleeping quarters, and continued, "Apart from his pay, which is considerable, Fett demanded only one thing — an unaltered clone for himself. Pure genetic replication. No tampering with the structure to make it more docile, and no growth acceleration. Curious isn't it?"

"I would like to meet this Jango Fett," Obi-Wan said. *I would like it very, very much.*

"I would be most happy to arrange it for you," Taun We told him.

Their last stop, Lama Su said, would be the training ground. Obi-Wan followed him out onto a balcony. Thousands of men in identical white body armor were drilling in the courtyard below. *He said it was an army,* Obi-Wan thought numbly.

"Magnificent, aren't they?" Lama Su said proudly.

Slowly, Obi-Wan nodded, feeling very cold. *The only thing you can do with an army is fight a war.* But Jedi didn't fight wars; they worked to keep the peace and the laws of the Republic without fighting. Obi-Wan stared down at the endless lines of clones marching past, wishing Sifo-Dyas were still alive to explain.

CHAPTER 8

True to her promise, Taun We arranged for Obi-Wan to meet Jango Fett as soon as the tour of the clone factories was over. She escorted him there herself. Obi-Wan took careful note of their route through the corridors, and even more careful note of the locking mechanism on Fett's apartment door once they arrived.

A boy of about ten answered the door, and Obi-Wan blinked, surprised in spite of himself. The boy had the same dark, curly hair and strong features as the young clones he had seen in the training school, but his expression was sharper somehow, more aware. *This must be Jango Fett's unmodified clone,* Obi-Wan thought.

"Boba, is your father here?" Taun We asked. The boy studied them for a moment, then nodded warily. "May we see him?"

"Sure," Boba said, not moving. When he finally

stepped aside and let them in, Obi-Wan felt as if he had barely managed to pass some hidden test.

They stepped into a modest apartment that impressed Obi-Wan mainly by how ordinary it seemed. Looking more closely, he realized that the room was well organized as well as neat. Though Jango Fett must have lived here for at least ten years, Obi-Wan saw few personal items. *He's a bounty hunter; he never knows who might come after him, or when he might have to leave in a hurry.*

"Dad!" Boba called. "Taun We's here."

A man entered from the next room. Though he was instantly recognizable as related to the clones, he looked older than the oldest of them — somewhere in his thirties, Obi-Wan guessed — and he moved with an assurance that the clones could not match. A scar ran down one side of his face, but even without it, he would have looked hard and tough. He nodded at Taun We and eyed Obi-Wan suspiciously.

"Welcome back, Jango," Taun We said. "Was your trip productive?"

"Fairly," Jango said without taking his eyes from Obi-Wan.

"This is Jedi Master Obi-Wan Kenobi," Taun We went on. "He's come to check on our progress."

"That right?" Jango's expression was skeptical and his tone was cold.

Obi-Wan smiled disarmingly. "Your clones are very impressive. You must be very proud."

"I'm just a simple man, trying to make my way in the universe, Master Jedi," Jango replied.

"Aren't we all?" Obi-Wan asked.

Through the partially open door behind Jango, Obi-Wan noticed some body armor lying on the floor of the next room. Before he could get a good look at it, Jango moved slightly, blocking his view. "Ever make your way as far as Coruscant?" Obi-Wan asked. He moved slightly to one side, hoping to get a better look.

Jango moved again, hiding the door. "Once or twice."

"Recently?"

"Possibly."

"Then you must know Master Sifo-Dyas," Obi-Wan said.

"Boba, close the door," Jango said to the boy. He smiled stiffly at Obi-Wan as the boy complied. Then he asked Obi-Wan, "Master who?"

"Sifo-Dyas," Obi-Wan repeated. "Isn't he the Jedi who hired you for this job?"

"Never heard of him," Jango declared. "I was recruited by a man called Tyranus on one of the moons of Bogden."

"Sifo-Dyas told us to expect him," Taun We put in. "And he showed up just when your Jedi Master said he would. We have kept the Jedi's involvement a secret until your arrival, just as your Master requested."

Curious, Obi-Wan thought.

"Do you like your army?" Jango asked, the spite clear in his voice.

"I look forward to seeing them in action," Obi-Wan replied carefully.

Now the bounty hunter grinned nastily. "They'll do their job well," he said. "I'll guarantee it."

And just what do you think their job will be? But asking that might make the bounty hunter more wary than he already was, so Obi-Wan merely nodded. "Thanks for your time, Jango," he said cordially.

"Always a pleasure to meet a Jedi," Jango replied.

Wondering if he had imagined the sarcasm in the bounty hunter's voice, Obi-Wan left with Taun We. He made his farewells to Lama Su and let the Kaminoans lead him back to the platform where he had left his starfighter. The rain and wind outside were even worse than he'd remembered, but he pulled his cloak close about himself and pretended to fiddle with something until he sensed that those inside had left. When he was certain no one was watching, he signaled R4. He had to send a message to Master Yoda and Master Windu at once. They needed to know what he had discovered, and he needed their direction. The situation was much too complex to risk making a false step now.

* * *

In spite of Padmé's determination to forget about Anakin's kiss, she couldn't. The memory kept returning at odd moments during the day when Anakin looked at her — and sometimes, when he didn't look at her. She should, she thought, have been annoyed.

But she couldn't be annoyed when Anakin was in such an exuberantly cheerful mood. He teased her and made fun of her until she stopped talking about politics. He juggled fruit, adding piece after piece until there were too many and they all fell on his head. He made her laugh, over and over, and he laughed with her.

It felt good to have someone to laugh with. But by evening, as she and Anakin sat before a huge fire in the open hearth at the lodge, Padmé was wondering whether coming to the lake lodge had been such a good idea after all. *This was a good choice*, she told herself for the hundredth time. Remote, isolated, easy to see in all directions — everything she had said to Anakin was true. The lodge was perfect for security purposes.

Unfortunately, it was perfect for other things, as well. She couldn't pretend not to see it anymore: Anakin *did* care for her. And the more time she spent with him, especially here, where some of her happiest childhood memories were, the more she cared —

Stop that, she told herself firmly. *You have important work to do. You don't have time to fall in love*. But being firm didn't stop the empty feeling in her stomach, or keep her from feeling . . . happy when she saw him come around a corner unexpectedly. And it didn't erase the memory of that kiss —

She heard a rustle of movement and looked up as Anakin bent toward her. *He's going to kiss me again*, she thought, and even as she turned her head away, she knew she wanted him to. "Anakin, no," she said, and the words came out sad instead of firm and decisive.

Anakin looked at her. After a moment, he began to speak — softly, without the confidence she had become used to seeing in him.

"From the moment I met you, all those years ago, a day hasn't gone by when I haven't thought of you," he told her. "Now that I'm with you again, I'm in agony. The closer I get to you, the worse it gets. The thought of not being with you makes my stomach turn over — my mouth go dry. I feel dizzy. I can't breathe. I'm haunted by the kiss you should never have given me. My heart is beating, hoping that kiss will not become a scar. You are in my very soul, tormenting me. What can I do? I will do anything you ask."

Anything? Would you forget that kiss? Would you stop looking at me all the time, the way you do — let both of us get back to our jobs? Padmé knew she should say the words, but she couldn't force them out.

After a moment, Anakin went on, "If you are suffering as much as I am, tell me."

Padmé turned her head away. "I . . . I can't. We can't. It's just not possible."

"Anything's possible," Anakin said. The confidence was returning to his voice. "Padmé, please listen —"

"*You* listen," Padmé snapped. Why did she have to be wise for both of them? "We live in a real world. Come back to it. You're studying to become a Jedi Knight. I'm a Senator. If you follow your thoughts through to conclusion, they will take us to a place we cannot go — regardless of the way we feel about each other."

"Then you *do* feel something!" Anakin said exultantly.

Hadn't he heard anything else she'd said? "Jedi aren't allowed to marry," Padmé said slowly and clearly, as if she were speaking to the little boy she remembered, instead of to this handsome young man she — "You'd be expelled from the Order. I will not let you give up your future for me."

"You're asking me to be rational," Anakin said after a moment. "That is something I know I cannot do. Believe me, I wish I could wish my feelings away, but I can't."

"I am *not* going to give in to this," Padmé said, half to herself. "I have more important things to do than fall in love." But the words rang hollowly in her ears.

"It wouldn't have to be that way," Anakin said. "We . . . we could keep it a secret."

"Then we'd be living a lie," Padmé told him gently. "And one we couldn't keep up even if we wanted to. I couldn't do that. Could you, Anakin?" She stared at him, willing him to understand, to accept. "Could you live like that?"

There was a long silence, and she began to be afraid that he would not answer. Finally he said, "You're right." He looked into the flames, and added almost under his breath, "It would destroy us."

Padmé shivered. There was a frightening conviction in Anakin's last words. She should be satisfied, she told herself. But she could not shake the feeling that they hadn't settled anything.

The more of Obi-Wan's report Yoda heard, the more disturbing he found it. He sensed the same concern in Mace Windu. But they both waited patiently for Obi-Wan to finish — the hologram signal was weak, and neither of them wanted to risk missing a crucial detail.

"Do you think these cloners are involved in the plot to assassinate Senator Amidala?" Mace asked when Obi-Wan finished.

"No, Master," Obi-Wan said. "There appears to be no motive."

"Do not assume anything, Obi-Wan," Yoda said reprovingly. "Clear, your mind must be if you are to discover the real villain behind this plot."

"Yes, Master," Obi-Wan replied. "They say a Sifo-Dyas placed the order for the clones almost ten years ago. I was under the impression he was killed before that. Did the Council ever authorize the creation of a clone army?"

"No," Mace Windu said decisively. "Whoever placed that order did not have the authorization of the Jedi Council."

Important, this clone army was, certainly; but also a distraction. Yoda frowned. How to reconcile the two? "Into custody, take this Jango Fett," he told Obi-Wan at last. "Bring him here. Question him, we will."

"Yes, Master," Obi-Wan said. "I will report back when I have him."

The hologram faded. Mace Windu reached out and turned the receiver off. *Move carefully, we must,* Yoda thought. *Lose our way, we might, in this maze of possibilities and deception.*

Padmé did not sleep well that night. Toward morning, she heard muffled cries from Anakin's room, but they stopped before she had to decide whether to go in or not. Another nightmare, she supposed.

She woke early and decided to sit on the balcony for a while before breakfast. Fresh air was just what she needed to clear her head. As she started out onto the balcony, she realized that Anakin was there before her. She hadn't noticed him at first because he was cross-legged on the floor, meditating. Quietly, she turned to leave.

"Don't go."

Padmé glanced back. Anakin's eyes were still closed, and he did not appear to have moved at all. "I don't want to disturb you," she said uncertainly.

"Your presence is soothing," Anakin assured her.

That's nice, Padmé thought. *But I don't think I can just stand here and be soothing for very long.* "You had a nightmare again last night," she said after a moment.

"Jedi don't have nightmares," Anakin said bitterly.

"I heard you."

Anakin opened his eyes and looked at her, and she could see in them all the torment he was feeling. "I saw my mother. I saw her as clearly as I see you now." He swallowed hard. "She's suffering, Padmé. They're killing her! She is in pain. . . ."

Stunned by the conviction in his voice, Padmé said nothing as Anakin rose to his feet. He closed his eyes again for a moment, as if he could not quite bear to look at her. Then he opened them and said miserably, "I know I'm disobeying my mandate to protect you, Senator. I know I will be punished, and possibly thrown out of the Jedi Order. But I have to go. I have to help her." He looked down. "I'm sorry, Padmé," he finished barely above a whisper. "I don't have a choice."

There has to be another choice, Padmé thought. She couldn't stand seeing him so wretched . . . and then she had it. "I'll go with you."

Anakin looked at her as if he could not make sense of what she had just said. Padmé held his eyes and continued, "That way, you can continue to protect me, and you won't be disobeying your mandate."

She still wasn't completely sure he had understood, until he took a deep breath and said, "What about Master Obi-Wan?"

Padmé sighed in relief; it was so good to see hope and determination take the place of his misery. A tiny part of her was frightened by the idea of having so much power over someone — a word or two was all it had taken to restore Anakin's confidence and good humor. Only a word or two, from her. She brushed the thought aside and smiled. Taking Anakin's hand, she said, "I guess we won't tell him, will we?"

CHAPTER 9

Obi-Wan shut down his transmitter. *Take Jango Fett into custody. Right.* He looked out at the torrents of rain pouring down just outside the protective canopy of his ship, and sighed. Then he pulled up his hood and opened the ship. Quietly, he slipped back into Tipoca City.

The Force let him sense and avoid the various people in the corridors, and he reached Jango Fett's apartment without incident. To his surprise, the door slid open at his touch, and he knew at once what he would find inside. The rooms were no longer neat and well organized. Empty drawers hung open, and the few personal items had vanished. *I knew he was ready to leave fast, but I didn't realize he could leave* this *fast!*

They couldn't have been gone long; it hadn't *been* that long since Obi-Wan had left them. He checked the wall computer and quickly tracked down the landing platform where Fett kept his ship. *Slave I — what an appropriate name for a bounty hunter's ship,* he thought when he read the platform listings. The ship was still there. Obi-Wan took just enough time to call up a map and find the shortest route to the platform. Then he left the apartment at a run.

The two Fetts were still loading their ship when he arrived. Jango was handing crates up to Boba. In his silver-gold body armor and jetpack, he was clearly the same man who had killed the assassin outside the nightclub. He had his back to the door, and Obi-Wan charged forward into the rain, hoping to surprise him. But the boy saw him coming and shouted, "Dad!"

Jango Fett drew his blaster as he turned. Obi-Wan pulled out his lightsaber just in time to deflect the blast. By then, he was almost on top of Fett, and he swung the lightsaber.

"Boba, get on board!" Jango shouted, and triggered his rockets. He shot up into the air, avoiding Obi-Wan's blow.

Obi-Wan spun as Jango flew over his head and landed behind him. The bounty hunter circled, firing toxic darts. Obi-Wan deflected them with the lightsaber. Though he aimed them back at Jango, the bounty hunter avoided most of them, and the rest bounced harmlessly off his armor.

Suddenly, the bounty hunter shot into the air again

and hovered out of reach. An instant later, a laser shell whizzed past Obi-Wan and blew a chunk out of the landing tower. The explosion threw Obi-Wan to the ground, knocking his lightsaber out of his hand. *The boy in the ship — he's firing at me!* So was Jango Fett, but Obi-Wan could deflect those shots with his lightsaber. That is, he could deflect them if he *had* his lightsaber.

Jango Fett landed just in front of him. Obi-Wan charged forward and grabbed him. *As long as we're close together, Boba can't fire without hitting his father.* But Jango used his rockets again, then kicked Obi-Wan loose in midair. Obi-Wan fell heavily and skidded across the smooth, wet surface, grabbing desperately for a handhold.

Just when he thought he had one, something flashed down and wrapped his wrists. *Clingwire!* Obi-Wan thought, and then he was being dragged rapidly toward a support column. Jango clearly meant to smash him against it, but Obi-Wan rolled sideways in time. He used his momentum to pull himself to his feet, then suddenly threw all of his weight against the wire.

The clingwire dug painfully into his wrists, but the sudden jerk brought Jango down. The bounty hunter lost his jetpack and slid off the flat landing area, down the slope toward the edge of the platform, pulling Obi-Wan with him. Faster and faster they went. Just as Jango Fett was about to slide off the edge, Obi-Wan saw claws extend from his armor to anchor him in place. Then, as he slid past Jango and over the edge, he sensed a flare of satisfaction from his opponent . . . and the wire around his wrists went slack.

Automatically, Obi-Wan grabbed hold of the loosened wire as he fell into the wind-whipped rain, feeling with the Force for the other end that Jango must have just released. For an eternal instant, he could not find it. Then he had it, and the Force sent it sideways among the great columns that supported the landing platform, to wrap around a cross beam. The wire cut into his hands again as he came to the end of it, but it was better than falling into the angry waves and being smashed against the support columns. He held on and swung under the landing platform.

Below him and a little ahead, he saw a small shelf — probably some sort of service platform — just above the waves. Thankfully, he let go of the wire and dropped onto it. Sure enough, there was a service door. Obi-Wan waved it open and charged up the stairs inside.

He arrived at the landing platform just as Fett's ship lifted to hover a few meters above the ground — the first step in takeoff. He barely had time to snatch a small magnetic tracker from his belt pouch and hurl it at the ship. Then *Slave I* took off, racing for the sky — but even through the pelting rain, Obi-Wan had heard the *clank* of the device attaching firmly to the ship's hull. With a relieved sigh, he picked up his lightsaber. All he had to do now was follow.

Tatooine hadn't changed. It was hot and dry — Anakin was surprised to find that he felt a little *too* hot; apparently, he was more used to cooler worlds now than he had realized. But the same motley collection of shady-looking beings made their way between the same blocky, sand-colored buildings, along the same packed-sand streets. He could have walked to Watto's junk shop blindfolded.

Yet he didn't feel . . . comfortable. Perhaps the problem was that he could see now how shoddy and backward this world was. He remembered how shocked Padmé had been to discover that he was Watto's slave; now he understood why.

Watto hadn't changed, either. The fat little Toydarian's first reaction to seeing a Jedi Padawan was "Whatever it is, I didn't do it!" But he seemed pleased to see Anakin, once he recognized him, and he was willing to help.

"Shmi's not mine no more," he told Anakin. "I sold her to a moisture farmer named Lars. I heard he freed her and *married* her. Can you beat that?"

Watto's trunklike nose wrinkled in evident amazement that anyone would pay good money for a slave in order to turn around and free her, no matter how he felt. "Long way from here — someplace over on the other side of Mos Eisley."

So Anakin and Padmé took the little Naboo starship they had borrowed and flew to Mos Eisley. The directions Watto had given them were easy enough to follow, and by late afternoon they were landing near a small homestead outside the city.

They left R2-D2 with the ship and started toward the buildings. A human-shaped droid straightened up from a condenser as they approached. "How may I be of service? I am See —"

"Threepio?" Anakin said, grinning and noticing that the Protocol Droid he had created now had coverings.

"Oh, my," said C-3PO, cocking his head to one side. "Oh, my maker! Master Anakin! I knew you would return."

"I've come to see my mother," Anakin told him.

C-3PO froze, as if his power had been suddenly disconnected. Anakin felt a sudden lump of fear in his throat. *Something is very wrong. I knew it.* C-3PO twitched and said, "I think — I think — Perhaps we'd better go indoors."

Anakin followed, torn between wanting to know what had happened and being afraid to hear what it was. C-3PO led them down to the sunken courtyard and introduced Anakin to Owen Lars and his girlfriend, Beru. Owen was a stocky young man who already had the quiet, solid look of a farmer; Beru had a practical air that was enhanced by the neat blonde braids that wrapped her head.

"I guess I'm your stepbrother," Owen said. "I had a feeling you might show up someday."

"Is my mother here?" Anakin burst out, unable to bear wasting more time being polite.

"No, she's not," said a grim voice.

Anakin turned. A small floating chair moved out of the main house. In it was a large older man who resembled Owen. One of his legs was wrapped in new bandages. The other leg was missing entirely.

"Cliegg Lars," the man said by way of introduction, extending one hand awkwardly. "Shmi is my wife. Come on inside. We have a lot to talk about."

Just tell me where Mom is! Anakin thought angrily, but he couldn't shout at a man in a float chair. So he followed Cliegg into the house, to the underground dining area. Beru served steaming cups of ardees while Cliegg began his story.

"It was just before dawn," he said, his voice hoarse with emotion. "They came out of nowhere. A hunting party of Tusken Raiders —"

Anakin's mind shut off. Tatooine was controlled by the Hutt criminal organization; it was a haven for smugglers, thieves, and other lowlifes. But even on Tatooine, the Tusken Raiders were considered vicious. They tortured people for fun, and they had his mother? He felt cold. *No, Mom, no . . .*

Cliegg was still talking. Anakin heard only snatches. "Thirty of us went out after her . . . I couldn't ride anymore . . . This isn't the way . . . been gone a month." Anakin forced his attention back to the present, just as Cliegg finished heavily, "There's little hope she's lasted this long."

You don't have my nightmares, Anakin thought. He stared around the table, seeing the shocked sympathy on Padmé's face, the hopeless grief on Cliegg's, the wary hope on Owen's. They all seemed far away, almost unreal, separated from him by the icy fear that had settled around his heart. Abruptly, he stood up.

"Where are you going?" Owen asked.

"To find my mother." He hardly heard Padmé's protest, or Cliegg's objections. "I can feel her pain, and I *will* find her."

They stared at him for a moment, then Owen said, "Take my speeder bike," and Anakin felt a distant warmth. Owen, at least, understood.

"I know she's alive," he said to that small, faraway understanding. Then he turned and went out. He'd seen a swoop bike near the stairs as they came down; that must be the one Owen meant.

As he reached the top of the steps, Padmé came running out. Before she could say anything, before she could ask him to let her come with him or, worse yet, ask him not to go, he said, "You are going to have to stay here. These are good people, Padmé. You'll be safe." She had to be safe. He needed to have something to come back to if . . . after he found his mother.

Padmé looked at him for a moment, and he was afraid she would argue, but she only said his name and hugged him. It almost cracked the ice that had settled around his heart. He wanted to smile at her, but he couldn't. "I won't be long," he said as he swung onto the swoop bike.

He started off across the desert. The noise of the speeder bike drowned out other sounds and the dusty wake behind it hid Padmé and the Lars homestead from sight almost immediately.

Hang on, Mom. I'm coming.

CHAPTER 10

Although the tracking device was working fine, Obi-Wan pushed his Delta-7 starfighter to top speed as he followed *Slave I*. He didn't want Jango Fett to get out of range. He had almost caught up when they reached a planetary system — the ship's databanks said it was called Geonosis — and the tracking signal vanished.

They seem to have discovered the tracker. Cautiously, Obi-Wan scanned the area. Fett had hidden in an asteroid belt. As soon as he realized Obi-Wan had found him again, he started releasing sonic charges. The two ships dodged and wove through the asteroids, firing at each other and trying to avoid a crash. *This is why I hate flying,* Obi-Wan thought, and then Fett connected and he was too busy struggling with the controls to think.

Fett's ship was larger and more heavily armed than Obi-Wan's; the next missile was a guided torpedo. Following Fett openly into the asteroid field had been a mistake, Obi-Wan decided as he swerved in and out among the asteroids in a vain attempt to lose the torpedo. It was time to try something tricky.

He picked out a large asteroid and headed straight into it at top speed. The torpedo followed mindlessly. "Arfour, prepare to jettison the spare parts canisters," Obi-Wan said as they approached. The little droid beeped acknowledgment. Obi-Wan relaxed into the Force, sensing for the exact right moment. "Release them now!" he commanded, and whipped the starfighter up and sideways.

The torpedo struck the asteroid behind him in a huge explosion that flung rock and the spare parts back into space. Obi-Wan ducked into one of the craters on the far side of the asteroid and shut down his power systems. With luck, Fett would be sure that the Jedi's ship had crashed and exploded, but Obi-Wan wasn't going to take chances. The bounty hunter might be clever enough to do a scan for power systems, just to make sure Obi-Wan's starfighter had really been destroyed.

He waited for what seemed like hours, then cautiously brought the power systems back up and took off. There was no sign of Jango Fett. With a relieved sigh, Obi-Wan sent his starfighter along Fett's last known route, down toward the planet of Geonosis.

Geonosis was a bare, rocky world. Dusty red

mesas baked by day and froze by night. R4's projection of Jango Fett's course took them to the night side. Obi-Wan saw no sign of cities, only huge stone spires that looked like stalagmites. *But stalagmites can only be built up inside, in caves,* Obi-Wan thought. *And it looks as if Fett was heading right for that one. Hmmm.*

At the edge of a small mesa near the stone spire, Obi-Wan found a rock ledge that stuck out far enough to hide his starfighter. Carefully, he maneuvered his ship into the gap underneath and landed. He double-checked his bearings, then started walking.

At the top of the trail, Obi-Wan paused. Pulling out a pair of electronic binoculars, he studied the plain around the strange spire. *Definitely not natural,* he thought, *and . . . what's that?* He brought the view back and saw a number of Trade Federation Core Ships parked in neat rows beside the spire. As he watched, a gap opened in the ground at one side as a lift platform dropped; a moment later, it returned, carrying row upon row of skeletal Battle Droids. *There must be a factory underground. I need to get a closer look.*

Sneaking into the spires was much easier than he had expected. The Core Ships and Battle Droids clustered around one side, probably the front; all Obi-Wan had to do was to climb up the back and slip in through a window. The interior was like a hive, full of narrow corridors that opened suddenly into huge spaces. Several times, he sensed someone coming barely in time to duck behind a pillar or into a doorway.

He reached a vast open area, high and wide and apparently deserted. As he was about to cross, he heard voices and darted behind a pillar.

A mixed group emerged from one of the corridors and started across the square. There were several tall, insectlike Geonosians and a number of off-worlders. Obi-Wan blinked in surprise as he recognized two of them: Nute Gunray, the Trade Federation Viceroy who had led the attack on Naboo ten years before, and the former Jedi, Count Dooku! He leaned forward to catch what they were saying.

"— persuade the Commerce Guild and the Corporate Alliance to sign the treaty," Count Dooku intoned.

"What about the Senator from Naboo?" Nute Gunray said, his wide mouth twisting. "Is she dead yet? I'm not signing your treaty until I have her head on my desk."

"I am a man of my word, Viceroy," Dooku replied.

Nute Gunray and Count Dooku are behind the assassination attempts! Padmé was right. Obi-Wan slipped through the shadows to the next pillar, hoping to get close enough to hear more, but one of the Geonosians began talking about the Battle Droids and then they passed through an arched doorway and out of earshot.

I need to find out what they're up to. Obi-Wan checked quickly to see if anyone else was coming, then crossed to a stairway next to the door. He was in luck; the stairs led to a long gallery overlooking the room below. Dooku seemed to be having a major conference; in addition to Nute Gunray and the Geonosians, Obi-Wan recognized several of the Senators who supported the Separatist movement, as well as representatives from the Commerce Guild and the Intergalactic Bank Clan.

As he listened to their conversation, Obi-Wan frowned. The Corporate Alliance and the Trade Federation — and their huge droid armies — were joining the Separatists. It looked as if Dooku really did mean to start a civil war. *Master Yoda must know about this at once,* Obi-Wan thought. He snuck back down the stairs and headed toward his ship.

It was after midnight when Anakin finally parked the speeder bike at the edge of a cliff overlooking the Tusken camp. He knew it was the right place. He had felt himself drawing nearer all night, just as he could feel his mother now in one of the hide-covered huts below. *Her pain* — he forced himself to stop trembling. *I'm almost there, Mom.*

Pulling his hood over his head, he crept down and into the camp. The Tusken Raiders had posted two guards at the front of the hut, but Anakin had never intended to walk in through the door. Carefully, he made his way through the shadows to the back of the hut. After checking to make sure no one was near, he lit his lightsaber.

The hide wall gave way quickly, and in a few moments he was inside. Moonlight fell through the smoke-hole in the roof, making it just possible to see the spent candles that littered the floor, the wooden frame in the center of the hut . . . and the figure of a woman hanging from the frame.

Without conscious thought, Anakin swung his lightsaber, and the ropes that held her parted. Dropping the weapon, he caught her as she fell. Even in the moonlight, he could see bruises on her face and arms; her eyes were swollen almost shut, and there was blood — he couldn't look at the blood, he wouldn't see it. "Mom," he said desperately. "Mom!"

His mother's eyes opened. "Annie?" she said in a faint, hoarse voice. "Is it you?"

Anakin choked, feeling the pain of her injuries even more clearly now that he was holding her. *She's . . . she's . . . I have to get her home!* "I'm here, Mom," he said urgently. "You're safe. Hang on." *Please, please hang on!* "I'm going to get you out of here."

But Shmi didn't seem to hear his words. Her eyes had finally focused on his face, and her battered features relaxed in an expression of tenderness. "Annie?

You look so handsome. My son . . . my grown-up son." She gasped and went on with evident difficulty. "I'm so proud of you, Annie. So proud." Her voice grew fainter; Anakin had to strain to hear the words. "I missed you so much. Now I am complete."

"Just stay with me, Mom," Anakin begged. The icy fear was closing around his heart again. "I'm going to make you well again. Everything's going to be fine." He reached for the Force as he spoke; surely he could do something that would help, that would ease the terrible pain he felt in her, that would give strength back to the life he could feel fading away between his arms. Something that would give her more time. The Force was there, but he didn't know how to use it for this.

Shmi tried to smile at him. She whispered, "I love . . ." and went horribly, finally still.

Anakin stared at her numbly. After a moment, he reached over and closed her eyes. *The Tusken Raiders did this. Animals, Cliegg called them — they're worse than animals. They're . . . they're . . . vicious, mindless, murdering* things. *I'll show them! I'll get them all!*

Oh, Mom. Mom . . .

CHAPTER 11

After worrying through most of the night, Padmé heard Beru shouting outside. "He's back! He's back!" She ran outside in time to see Anakin land the swoop bike. *He's all right!* she thought, and then she saw his face as he lifted his mother's body from the bike, and wondered if he would ever be all right again.

Anakin said nothing to anyone; he took Shmi's body inside the homestead and then went out to the workroom alone. *He is in pain,* Padmé thought. She frowned in worry at the closed workroom door for a long time. Then she went to the kitchen and set up a tray of food. If Anakin wouldn't come out, she'd go in after him.

When she carried the tray into the workroom, Anakin was fiddling with a welder and some parts. He didn't look up.

"I brought you something," Padmé said.

Anakin stayed bent over the workbench. "The

shifter broke," he said in a tense voice that she hardly recognized. "Life seems so much simpler when you're fixing things." His face tightened. "I'm *good* at fixing things. But I couldn't —" He slammed the parts down on the bench and looked up, and Padmé saw tears in his eyes. "Why did she have to die?" he demanded. "Why couldn't I save her? I know I could have!"

"Sometimes there are things no one can fix," Padmé said gently. "You're not all-powerful, Annie."

"I should be!" Anakin said, suddenly angry. "Someday I *will* be! I will be the most powerful Jedi ever! I will even learn to stop people from dying."

Padmé could feel the emotions swirling around him: hurt, frustration, anger, grief . . . and fear. It frightened her, but she didn't know what to do about it. Uncertainly, she said, "Anakin —"

"It's all Obi-Wan's fault!" Anakin shouted. "He's jealous! He knows I'm already more powerful than he is. He's holding me back!" He hurled his wrench across the room, and Padmé stared, shocked. His hands were trembling; he looked at them as if they belonged to someone else.

This isn't just about his mother. There's something else going on. Padmé took a deep breath. "Annie, what's wrong?"

"I — I killed them," Anakin whispered, and Padmé went cold. "I killed them all. They're dead, every single one of them. Not just the men. The women and the children, too." He looked up at last, his face working, and Padmé had to force herself not to back away from the look in his eyes. "They're like animals," he spat, "and I slaughtered them like animals. I hate them!" Then the angry mask crumbled away, and he broke into sobs.

Without thinking, Padmé stepped forward and cradled him in her arms. Part of her was still shocked and horrified — *Women and children? My Anakin killed them all?* — and she knew she ought to tell him so. But she couldn't bear to add to his grief.

"Why do I hate them?" Anakin stammered between sobs. "I didn't — I couldn't — I couldn't control myself. I don't want to hate them . . . but I just can't forgive them."

"To be angry is to be human," Padmé said.

"To control your anger is to be a Jedi." Anakin sounded lost, and she could feel him shaking. *That's it — he's afraid they'll tell him he can't be a Jedi,* she thought. *But Jedi aren't superhuman. He knows he shouldn't have done this. They'll understand.*

"Shhh," she told him, rocking him gently.

"No," Anakin argued, "I'm a Jedi. I know I'm better than this. I'm sorry — I'm so sorry."

"You're human. You're like everyone else. Shhhh."

She stayed with him for a long time, then made him eat something. He seemed to her so brittle that a harsh word would break him, and she did not want to leave him alone. Near noon, Beru came to tell them that Owen and the homestead's droids had finished digging Shmi's grave, and they went out to the simple burial.

The ceremony did not take much time. Cliegg made a short speech, and Owen and C-3PO lowered Shmi's body into the grave. Cliegg looked down, tears running across his face. "You were the most loving partner a man could ever have," he said. "Goodbye, my dearest wife, and thank you."

Anakin stepped forward and knelt for a moment at the side of the grave. In a low voice, he said, "I wasn't strong enough to save you, Mom, but I promise I won't fail again." Then, in a whisper that only Padmé was near enough to hear, he added, "I miss you so much."

The silence that followed was broken by a string of beeps and whistles. Padmé turned angrily and saw R2-D2 rolling toward them. "Artoo, what are you doing here?"

C-3PO stepped forward. "It seems that he is carrying a message from someone called Obi-Wan Kenobi," the Protocol Droid translated. "Does that mean anything to you, Master Anakin?"

Padmé looked at Anakin uncertainly, but he only nodded and rose to his feet. They made a hasty farewell to the Lars homestead, and Owen told

Anakin to take C-3PO with him. Then they all hurried back to Padmé's starship to play Obi-Wan's message.

The recording started calmly enough, with a request to retransmit the message to Coruscant. Padmé made the proper connections and they settled back to watch.

The news was grim. Obi-Wan had found the assassin, but he had also stumbled across a secret alliance between Count Dooku and the Commerce Guilds. "They have both pledged their armies to Count Dooku," the little image of Obi-Wan said, "and are forming an — Wait! What!"

Padmé jerked upright in her seat as the recording showed Obi-Wan being attacked by droidekas, the Trade Federation's rolling Security Droids. Anakin jumped out of his chair and began pushing buttons, but no matter how he tried, he could not make contact with Obi-Wan again. Then he tried Coruscant. He got through quickly, but the response was not reassuring.

"We will deal with Count Dooku," Jedi Master Mace Windu told them. "The most important thing for you, Anakin, is to stay where you are." He frowned sternly. "Protect the Senator at all costs. That is your first priority."

"Understood, Master," Anakin replied in a dull tone.

"They'll never get there in time," Padmé burst out as the hologram shut off. "They have to come half-way across the galaxy. Look, Geonosis is less than a parsec away."

"You heard Master Windu," Anakin said in the same dead voice. "He gave me strict orders to stay here."

You told me before that Obi-Wan was like a father to you — and you just lost your mother. You can't just let him die. Padmé pressed her lips together to keep from speaking the hurtful words. *And Obi-Wan is my friend, too.* She reached out and flicked the flight preparation switches on the starship's cockpit. "He gave you strict orders to protect me," she said, "and I'm going to save Obi-Wan. So if you plan to protect me, you will have to come along."

For a moment, Anakin stared at her uncertainly. Then he gave her a wobbly grin and took the controls.

I hope we're in time, Padmé thought as the starfighter rose from Tatooine. *We have to be in time.*

The Geonosian prison cell was not particularly uncomfortable; it was just that the energy field in which Obi-Wan was suspended did not allow him any movement. There was a crackle, and a sharp, tingly pain shot through his arm. *Oh, yes, and the electric restraints are definitely unpleasant.*

He must have gotten careless on his way back to

the starfighter, he thought. If the Geonosians or anyone else had spotted him while he was eavesdropping on the meeting, they'd have stopped him before he got his message off. He hoped Anakin had retransmitted it without doing anything harebrained. Anything *else* harebrained, he amended; what *was* the boy doing on Tatooine? If Obi-Wan hadn't thought to widen the signal when he couldn't raise Anakin on Naboo, he would never have gotten his message through. . . .

The door of the cell opened, and Count Dooku walked in. If he could have moved, Obi-Wan would have stiffened.

"Hello, my friend," the Count said. "This is a mistake, a terrible mistake. They've gone too far. This is madness."

"I thought you were their leader, Dooku," Obi-Wan said, trying not to wince as the electric restraints crackled again.

"This had nothing to do with me, I assure you," Dooku said in a sincere-sounding tone. "I promise you, I will petition immediately to have you set free."

He can't know what I saw, Obi-Wan thought. In what he hoped was a casual tone, he said, "Well, I hope it doesn't take too long. I have work to do."

"It's a great pity that our paths have never crossed before, Obi-Wan," Dooku went on. "Qui-Gon always spoke very highly of you. I wish he were still alive."

So do I. Obi-Wan suppressed the pang of grief he

still felt when he thought of his Master, killed by a Sith Lord during the Naboo war ten years before.

"I could use his help right now," Dooku continued, watching Obi-Wan narrowly.

Despite himself, Obi-Wan stiffened. "Qui-Gon Jinn would *never* join you."

"Don't be so sure, my young Jedi," Dooku said gently. "He was once my apprentice, just as you were once his. He knew all about the corruption in the Senate, but we would never have gone along with it if he had known the truth as I have."

"The truth?" What truth could justify starting a civil war?

"What if I told you that the Republic was now under the control of the Dark Lords of the Sith?"

"No," Obi-Wan said. "That's not possible. The Jedi would be aware of it." *But a Sith Lord killed Qui-Gon . . . and Master Yoda said there are always two. Where has the other one been these ten years?*

"The dark side of the Force has clouded their vision, my friend," Dooku said sadly. "Hundreds of Senators are now under the influence of a Sith Lord called Darth Sidious."

Obi-Wan tried to reach out with the Force to sense the truth of what Dooku was saying, but the electric restraints crackled again and he could not maintain his concentration. "I don't believe you," he told Dooku.

"The Viceroy of the Trade Federation was once in

league with this Darth Sidious, but he was betrayed. He came to me for help. The Jedi Council would not believe him. I've tried many times to warn them, but they wouldn't listen to me." Dooku leaned forward, almost touching the force field. "You must join me, Obi-Wan, and together we will destroy the Sith."

Obi-Wan stared. Dooku's claims about the Senate and the Sith Lord were deeply disturbing — but the fact remained that Dooku had plotted with that same Trade Federation Viceroy to assassinate Senator Amidala, and he was preparing to start a civil war that could tear the galaxy apart. *I am a Jedi. I will not be a party to such things.* "I will never join you, Dooku."

Dooku studied him for a moment, then shook his head. As he turned to leave, he said casually, "It may be difficult to secure your release." Then he was gone.

The message was clear: *Join me, or you stay here.* Hung up in a force field with electric restraints, with no chance to escape and report what he had learned — Obi-Wan tried to shake his head, but the energy field kept it from moving. Maybe he should pretend to join Dooku; then as soon as they let him out, he could . . . but no, that wouldn't work. Dooku had been a Jedi. He would sense Obi-Wan's true purpose.

And what if Dooku had told the truth? If the Senate

was under the control of the Sith, if the Jedi Council had ignored his warnings . . . But surely Master Yoda would not do such a thing.

Obi-Wan stared at the closed door, feeling very much alone.

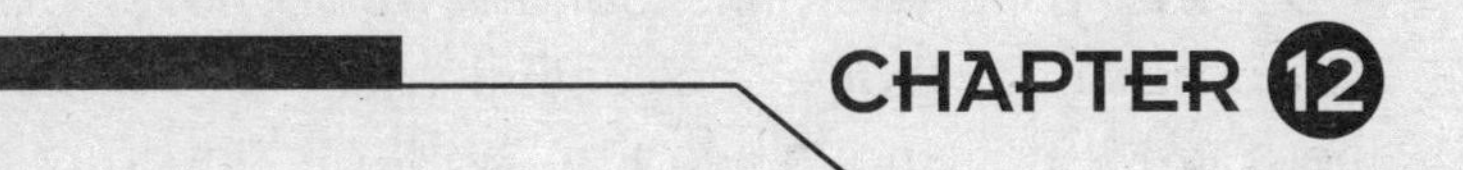

CHAPTER 12

As Obi-Wan's message finished playing, Yoda frowned. He could sense the shock in the other members of the Jedi Council as Obi-Wan spoke of the treachery of the Trade Federation. *But incomplete was Obi-Wan's report,* Yoda thought. He looked at Mace Windu. "More happening on Geonosis, I feel, than has been revealed," he said.

"I agree," Mace said.

Their first step was to contact Chancellor Palpatine, for the threat to the Republic was plainly greater than anyone had thought. They met in the Chancellor's office, along with the loyalist Senators who supported Palpatine.

Everyone listened carefully to Mace Windu's summary; then Bail Organa shook his head. "The Commerce Guilds are preparing for war — there can be no doubt of that."

Yoda's ears twitched. Listen, these Senators did not. They feared, and reacted. They did not *think*.

"Now we *need* that clone army!" Senator Ask Aak burst out.

But everyone knew the Senate would never give its approval for that — not until it was too late. And there were not enough Jedi to hold off an army of droids.

"Through negotiation, the Jedi maintains peace," Yoda said pointedly. "To start a war, we do not intend." There might, even yet, be time to talk a way out of the conflict . . . but he sensed no patience in the room, only fear and urgency as the Senators discussed what to do.

"The Senate must vote the Chancellor emergency powers," Mas Amedda suggested at last. "Then he could approve the use of the clones."

War, you mean, Yoda thought sadly. What other use was there for an army? Not in centuries had Yoda so wanted to comment, to interfere in the politics playing out before him, but he had already said what was needed, and the Senators had not grasped his meaning. He held his peace. *Jedi serve. Make laws, we do not.*

The Senators looked at one another. Plainly, they thought the idea was a good one, but none of them wanted to be the one to propose such a huge change in the way the government ran. Finally, Jar Jar Binks stepped forward.

"Mesa proud to proposing the motion to give

yousa honor emergency powers," he said to Palpatine, and the matter was quickly settled. Jar Jar would bring the motion up, and the other Senators would support it. When it passed, Chancellor Palpatine would approve the emergency use of the clone army.

Barely an hour later, Yoda sat beside Mace Windu, looking down from the visitors' balcony as the Senate seethed. The news had leaked out; he could feel the fear hanging over the chamber like dense fog. *Fear is the path to the dark side*, he thought, but the Senate would not understand even if there were some way he could tell them.

With almost indecent haste, the motion to give Chancellor Palpatine full emergency powers was proposed and passed. The Senate cheered Jar Jar's courage, and Palpatine rose to speak.

"It is with great reluctance that I have agreed to this," the Chancellor said. "The power you give me, I will lay down when this crisis has abated. And as my first act with this new authority, I will create a grand army of the Republic to counter the increasing threats of the Separatists."

Yoda shook his head sadly. Beside him, Mace Windu stirred. "It is done, then," he said heavily. He looked at Yoda. "I will take what Jedi we have left and go to Geonosis to help Obi-Wan."

That left the other task to him. Yoda nodded, accepting it. "Visit I will the cloners on Kamino, and see what it is they are creating." *And to see whether there still is some way this war to avoid.*

Piloting the Naboo starship to Geonosis was easy. Too easy; Anakin still felt shaken and unsure, and he wanted a job that would keep him too busy to think. Fear coiled around his heart: fear that he would lose control again; fear that Obi-Wan was already dead; fear that Obi-Wan was alive and would despise him when he learned what Anakin had done. It was no good telling himself that Obi-Wan was a Jedi and Jedi didn't hate. *I'm a Jedi, and I hate those Tusken Raiders.*

The thought made his stomach clench, and brought back the bloody scene at the camp. He fought back tears, unable to say whether they were tears of remorse or hatred. To distract himself, he leaned over the instrument panel. Perhaps there was some way to get to Geonosis faster . . .

Dragging every possible bit of speed out of the starship kept Anakin's mind occupied for the rest of the trip. When they reached the planet at last, R2-D2 pinpointed the area where Obi-Wan's transmission had originated, and they headed for it. Anakin kept the ship close to the ground, partly to keep from being detected and partly because dodging the many rock formations kept his mind fully occupied. Padmé looked for a place to hide the starship.

"See those columns of steam straight ahead?"

Padmé said suddenly, pointing. "They're exhaust vents of some type."

"That'll do," Anakin said, and sent the starship down one of them. He landed at the bottom. As he shut the engines down, Padmé turned toward him.

"Look, whatever happens out there, follow my lead," she told him. "I'm not interested in getting into a war here. Maybe I can find a diplomatic solution to this mess."

"Don't worry," Anakin said, forcing a grin. "I've given up trying to argue with you." But he couldn't help wondering whether she thought he *needed* the warning, after what he'd done on Tatooine.

R2 whistled plaintively as Anakin and Padmé left the ship. Preoccupied, Anakin nodded at the droids; most of his mind was concentrated on sensing the Force, searching for life-forms that they should avoid.

The tall underground corridors seemed empty, but Anakin felt uncomfortable. His unease grew as they went farther into the city. Finally, he stopped. "Wait," he called to Padmé, and concentrated. There was something . . . behind; behind and *above* . . .

Anakin's lightsaber leaped into his hands, and he whirled just as a large, insectlike creature swooped down on him. He cut it down, but more were coming. Padmé dashed through a door at the end of the corridor. Anakin cut down three more of the creatures and followed.

They found themselves on a narrow walkway

above some sort of factory, full of droids and conveyer belts and noisy machinery. The door slid shut behind them, and the walkway began to retract. A moment later, more of the winged creatures poured into the area.

Anakin readied his lightsaber while Padmé tried to open the door, but there was no switch on their side. The ledge they stood on grew narrower. Padmé looked at Anakin, then at the retreating walkway — and then, to his horror, she jumped off.

"Padmé!" Anakin cried, and leaped after her. She had landed on one of the conveyor belts, and was already well ahead of him. He started toward her, but the winged creatures attacked and he had to stop to fight them off.

One of the flying things attacked Padmé. Frantic to get to her, Anakin slashed at the creatures surrounding him, but more and more of them kept coming, blocking him. From the corner of his eye, he saw her fall into a huge empty vat, one of a line moving along another conveyor belt. *At least these things can't get at her in there,* Anakin thought, cutting several more creatures in half. And then he saw where the vat was headed — toward a huge cauldron to be filled with molten iron.

Padmé! The vat was too deep and smooth for her to climb out. *She'll be killed — no, Padmé, please, no . . .* As he struggled to reach her through the clouds of flying attackers, he saw a squat, cylindrical shape fly past on rocket jets. A tiny part of his mind wondered what R2-D2 was doing there, but he was too busy fighting to do more than notice the little droid. *Padmé . . .*

His foot slipped. Anakin fell sideways and landed on a molding device. He slid, and his arm caught in the machine. Slowly, it pulled him toward an enormous cutter. He struggled, but to no avail. *No! I have to get to Padmé!*

A triumphant whistle pierced the din. *That sounded like R2.* Anakin craned his neck, and saw one of the vats tip over just before it reached the filling station. Padmé rolled out of it onto a walkway. *R2 must have reprogrammed the controlling computer,* he thought, and then the cutter came down just ahead of him. He had to reserve all his attention for his own plight.

He twisted, trying to get himself out of the way of the cutter. His lightsaber was in the hand that was caught; he switched it on, hoping to be able to turn it enough to free himself in time.

The cutting blade came down again, smashing the lightsaber. The next strike would take off his arm . . . and then the machines froze.

Anakin looked up. He was surrounded by droidekas. Farther down, he saw Padmé, also surrounded. An armored figure dropped from the ceiling on a jetpack — *that's the bounty hunter we were looking for!* — and pointed a blaster at him.

"Don't move, Jedi!" the bounty hunter said.

So much for rescuing Obi-Wan, Anakin thought bitterly. *I couldn't save my mom, either, and now I've brought Padmé right to the people who've been trying to kill her. I've failed at everything.*

When the Geonosians did not kill them at once, Padmé's mind began working rapidly. By the time the guards led her and Anakin into a large conference room, she was calm and ready. As they entered, she saw Count Dooku sitting at a large table. The bounty hunter stood behind him, and there were Geonosian guards everywhere, even though the first thing their captors had done was to confiscate their weapons. *They certainly aren't taking any chances*, she thought.

Before anyone else could speak, Padmé stepped forward. "You are holding a Jedi Knight, Obi-Wan Kenobi," she said in her best Senatorial voice. "I am formally requesting that you turn him over to me. Now."

Count Dooku studied her calmly. "He has been convicted of espionage, Senator," he said. "And he will be executed. In just a few hours, I believe." He smiled gently, as if the thought pleased him.

"He is an officer of the Republic!" Padmé said, outraged. "You can't do that!"

"We don't recognize the Republic here, Senator," the Count replied, and smiled again. "But . . . if Naboo were to join our Alliance —"

So that was his game. She was Naboo's official representative in galactic matters; in some ways, she had as much power as the Queen. If she committed Naboo to the Separatists, her planet and her Queen would be bound by her decision. She listened with half an ear to the Count's smooth arguments, thinking, *I can't betray my planet and my principles, not even for Obi-Wan, not even for Anakin.* She couldn't see Anakin; he was standing behind her, and she was almost glad. She wasn't sure she could bear to look at him right now. *Oh, Anakin, I'm sorry I got you into this.*

Finally, she looked at the Count and said clearly, "I will not forsake all I have honored and worked for. I will not betray the Republic."

The Count sighed. "Then you will betray your Jedi friends? Without your cooperation, I can do nothing to stop their execution."

"And what about me?" Padmé asked, raising her chin.

"There are individuals who have a strong interest in your demise, M'lady," the Count said. "It has nothing to do with politics; it's purely personal."

Nute Gunray of the Trade Federation, Padmé thought. *Obi-Wan's message said he was behind the assassination attempts. He hates me because I led the successful counterattack when he invaded Naboo ten years ago.*

"I'm sure they will push hard to have you included

in the executions," the Count continued. "Without your cooperation, I've done all I can for you."

The Count sat back in his chair, and the bounty hunter waved to the guards. "Take them away," he said in a harsh voice.

The Geonosian guards took them to separate holding cells, and Padmé had time to think. The more she thought, the more certain she became that they were going to die. The Jedi knew Obi-Wan was on Geonosis, but they couldn't move without authorization from the Senate, and she had served in the Senate long enough to know that it would take days of debate before the Senators would agree to such a ticklish rescue mission. She didn't think the Geonosians would wait that long.

She was right. A few hours later, she and Anakin were brought to a large courtroom. The Archduke of Geonosis and his aide stood in the judge's box; to one side, Padmé saw Count Dooku, along with several Senators who she knew supported the Separatists. Beside them stood representatives from most of the Commerce Guilds, the Trade Federation, and the Intergalactic Bank Clan.

The Geonosians got right to the point. "You have been charged and found guilty of espionage," said one, and before they could respond, the Archduke asked, "Do you have anything to say before your sentence is carried out?"

"You are committing an act of war, Archduke," Padmé said. "I hope you are prepared for the consequences."

The Archduke laughed. "We build weapons, Senator; that is our business! Of course we're prepared." He waved at the guards. "Take them to the arena!"

Padmé's faint hope vanished. The guards dragged them out of the room and down to a dimly lit tunnel, where they were tied to the sides of a small, open cart. Miserably, Padmé looked across at Anakin. *This is all my fault. I insisted on coming, and now I've gotten us both killed.*

"Don't be afraid," Anakin said earnestly. He seemed more worried about her than about himself.

"I'm not afraid to die," Padmé told him. She looked down. If ever there was a time for truth, this was it. She couldn't lie to herself anymore, and she certainly couldn't lie to Anakin, not even by keeping silent. "I've been dying a little bit each day since you came back into my life."

Anakin's eyes widened, and he went very still. "What are you talking about?" he asked, as if he wasn't quite sure of what he had just heard.

Well, she would make it clear. "I love you," she said.

"You love me?" Anakin sounded as if he didn't know whether to be outraged or elated. "I thought we decided not to fall in love. That we would be forced to live a lie. That it would destroy our lives —"

Yes, we said all those things. But this turns out to be something that I can't just decide rationally. "I think our lives are about to be destroyed anyway," she said. Groping for the right words, she went on slowly, "My love for you is a puzzle, Annie, for which I have no answers. I can't control it — and now I don't care." She looked directly into his eyes, wishing she could touch him once more. But they were tied to opposite sides of the cart, and she couldn't reach him. "I truly, deeply love you, and before we die I want you to know."

Anakin's lips trembled. Slowly, hesitantly, he leaned forward. Padmé stretched toward him, and for the second time their lips met.

And then the cart jerked forward, throwing them both off balance. As Padmé regained her feet, she heard the roar of a crowd, growing louder and nearer. A moment later, they came out of the tunnel into the execution arena.

CHAPTER 13

Obi-Wan leaned against the execution post in the center of the Geonosian arena and once more tested the chains that held his arms over his head. What were the Geonosians waiting for? They'd had him out here for half an hour already, and the crowd was getting restless. Not that Obi-Wan was in any particular hurry . . .

The crowd roared, and Obi-Wan looked up. A small cart was pulling into the arena, and when he saw its passengers, Obi-Wan sighed and closed his eyes momentarily. *I knew Anakin was going to do something else harebrained, I just knew it.*

But there was no point in scolding Anakin now, and from the look on his face, there was no need to. Obi-Wan waited while the Geonosians chained Anakin to the post next to him. From the corner of his eye, he saw Padmé slip something small into her mouth behind the guards' backs just before they turned and chained her to the post beside Anakin.

"I was beginning to wonder if you'd gotten my message," Obi-Wan said as the guards started out of the arena.

"I retransmitted it just as you requested, Master," Anakin said earnestly. His neck muscles twitched, as if he was trying not to look at Padmé. "Then we decided to come and rescue you."

Obi-Wan glanced up at his chained hands. "Good job!"

In the stands, he saw Nute Gunray and the other trade and commercial delegates crowding into a large luxury box with the Geonosian Archduke. Count Dooku was near the front, along with his bounty hunter bodyguard. As soon as the cart left the arena, the Archduke made a formal announcement that Obi-Wan, Anakin, and Padmé were to be killed — as if anyone in the arena hadn't known that — and then declared loudly, "Let the executions begin!"

The crowd roared again, even more loudly than before, and three large gates opened on the far side of the arena. From the first gate came an enormous, broad-shouldered beast with great horns. *A reek*, Obi-Wan thought. *Powerful, but stupid.* Through the second gate came a gigantic catlike creature with long fangs — a nexu — and the third gate disgorged an acklay, which was a starfighter-sized lizard equipped with pincers large enough to chop a man in half. Behind each of the monsters came a horde of

Geonosian picadors riding smaller beasts and carrying long spears.

The picadors prodded the three monsters toward the center of the arena. "I've got a bad feeling about this," Anakin said.

"Take the one on the right," Obi-wan said, nodding at the reek. "I'll take the one on the left."

"What about Padmé?" Anakin asked.

Obi-Wan looked past Anakin and smiled slightly. Padmé had picked the lock on one of her restraints — *So that's what she was hiding from the guards! A lock pick!* — and used the chain as a rope to climb to the top of her post. She was balanced there, alternately fiddling with the remaining handcuff and pulling at the chain to loosen it from the pillar. "She seems to be on top of things," Obi-Wan said dryly.

Startled, Anakin glanced toward Padmé. Then he gave Obi-Wan a grin that held only a trace of the cockiness Obi-Wan remembered in his apprentice.

What happened *to him?* Obi-Wan thought, and then the monsters charged.

The acklay headed straight for Obi-Wan, its pincers open wide. *Those things are nearsighted*, Obi-Wan thought. *If I time this right* . . . Just before the acklay reached him, he dodged behind the post.

The acklay continued its charge. Its pincer closed around the execution post, right where the Jedi should have been, and the post splintered. Obi-Wan yanked the restraining chain free and glanced quickly around.

Anakin had jumped on the reek's back and looped the chain that held him around one of the reek's horns. The reek was shaking its head and straining against the chain; it wouldn't take much longer to pull the restraints free. The nexu was trying to climb the pole to get at Padmé. As Obi-Wan watched, she swung down on the chain and struck it with both feet, knocking it back. *Padmé can take care of herself — for a while.*

The acklay finished reducing the pole to splinters. Shaking its head, it peered around as if hunting for the tasty tidbit that it knew should have been in there somewhere. It saw Obi-Wan and started forward again.

Obi-Wan ran for the edge of the arena, where the picadors with their long spears were grouped. Startled, one of the riding beasts reared. While the picador was busy trying to deal with his mount, Obi-Wan grabbed the end of his spear and jerked it out of his hands. Planting the far end, he let his momentum and the long spear carry him up and over the picador.

Close behind him, the acklay slammed into the riding beast, knocking the picador off. The Geonosian screamed once before the acklay's pincer closed around him. The other picadors scattered before the acklay's charge, but they would be back soon enough. *One thing at a time,* Obi-Wan thought. The picador's spear wasn't much of a weapon, but it might be enough if he could hit the beast in the right place. He aimed and threw.

The spear caught the acklay in the side of its neck. The acklay screeched, dropped the picador's body, and charged. *Well, that didn't help much,* Obi-Wan thought, ducking behind the dead picador's riding beast.

The acklay followed him, but more slowly than it had before. Obi-Wan kept ahead of it, but he couldn't widen the gap between them. Then he saw the reek coming toward him — with Anakin and Padmé on its back, and the nexu bounding angrily after it. Anakin seemed to have found a way to steer the creature with the aid of the Force. Obi-Wan leaped up.

He landed behind Padmé. Glancing over his shoulder, he saw the nexu attack the wounded acklay. *That's two of them out of the way, for a while. If we can —*

Gates opened all around the arena, and droidekas rolled out. They circled the reek and uncoiled, activating their shields and bringing their powerful blasters to bear. The reek snorted and shook its head, turning in circles to avoid the Security Droids, but the droidekas were everywhere. *We're dead. Why haven't they started firing?*

A sudden silence fell. Obi-Wan looked up at the

crowd and his eyes widened. All over the arena, blue and green lightsabers flared. *There must be at least a hundred Jedi up there!* He glanced toward the archducal box and his jaw dropped. At this distance, he couldn't make out the features of the man in the Jedi robes standing next to Count Dooku — but he didn't have to. Only one Jedi carried a purple lightsaber. *Master Windu!*

As the reek carrying Anakin, Padmé, and Obi-Wan bounded past the archducal box, Count Dooku suppressed a smile. They were certainly an inventive group, but their tricks would make no difference in the long run.

Beside him, Viceroy Nute Gunray turned angrily. "This isn't how it's supposed to be! Jango, finish her off!"

Dooku motioned for Fett to stay where he was. Really, the Neimoidian was almost as entertaining as the Jedi. "Patience, Viceroy," Dooku said to Nute with a slight smile. "She will die."

The Viceroy snorted and turned back to the arena. Amusing as it was to watch his frustration, it was time to end things. Dooku signaled surreptitiously, and his hidden droidekas poured from gates all around the arena. The crowd cheered and Nute Gunray sat back in satisfaction, but Dooku sensed only a feeling of chagrin from behind them where

Jango Fett was standing. He turned to see what his bodyguard had noticed.

Mace Windu stood next to Jango, his lightsaber glowing a clear purple. *The noise of the crowd must have covered the sound when he ignited it,* Dooku thought. He hid his surprise with an elegant nod of welcome. "Master Windu, how pleasant of you to join us. You're just in time for the moment of truth." He gestured at the arena. "I think these two new boys of yours could use a little more training."

Master Windu's grim expression did not change. "Sorry to disappoint you, Dooku," he said in a low, hard voice. "This party is over." He gestured, and all around the arena, lightsabers blazed to life.

Dooku curled his lips in a combination of amusement and pleasure. *This is going even better than I had hoped. There are over a hundred Jedi out there, plus Master Windu; we will kill them all.* "Brave, but foolish, my old Jedi friend," he said gently to Mace. "You're impossibly outnumbered."

"I don't think so," Master Windu snapped. "The Geonosians aren't warriors. One Jedi has to be worth a hundred Geonosians."

"It wasn't the Geonosians I was thinking about," Dooku said, allowing his smile to grow. "How well do you think one Jedi will hold up against a *thousand* Battle Droids?"

Even as he spoke, the first of the new Super Battle Droids appeared in the corridor behind Mace Windu.

They began firing immediately. Master Windu deflected the blasts easily, but to do so, he had to take his attention from the others in the archducal box. Immediately, Jango Fett raised his flamethrower and fired.

Master Windu dodged, but the flames caught the edge of his robe and set it on fire. As more Battle Droids flooded into the arena, he jumped over the wall to the sand below. Count Dooku shook his head at such stubborn foolishness and settled back to enjoy the mayhem. *Yes, this will be very interesting indeed.*

For a moment, seeing Master Windu, Obi-Wan felt relieved; then Battle Droids began pouring into the arena from all directions. The Geonosians fled as energy bolts began to fly. *So many droids! Can we —*

The reek bucked, and Obi-Wan went flying. He landed rolling and dodged an energy bolt. The droidekas were firing. He couldn't dodge all of them for very long. He needed a lightsaber.

As if in answer to his thoughts, a lightsaber came flying toward him. He caught it and activated it in one smooth movement, saluted the Jedi who'd tossed it to him, and deflected four energy bolts back toward Battle Droids. Anakin had a lightsaber now, too, he saw, and Padmé had found a blaster somewhere.

The fight was the worst Obi-Wan had ever been through. It was far worse than Naboo had been. The

Battle Droids kept coming and coming, endlessly. No matter how many they destroyed, there were always more. At one point, he found himself back-to-back with Mace Windu. They seemed to be making progress — and then Jango Fett rocketed down to join the fight. Mace went after the bounty hunter, and Obi-Wan was on his own again.

There are too many of them! Obi-Wan lost count of the droids he had destroyed. He could feel Jedi dying around him, overwhelmed by sheer numbers. The sand of the arena was soaked with blood and littered with droid parts, and more Battle Droids were still coming. The three execution-monsters were dead — Obi-Wan vaguely remembered killing the acklay himself — but that hardly seemed to matter.

Suddenly the droids stopped firing. Obi-Wan lowered his tired arms and looked around. Mace Windu, Padmé, Anakin, and about twenty Jedi stood in the center of the arena, surrounded by Battle Droids. *Only twenty!* he thought in shock. There must have been at least a hundred lightsabers shining in the arena when he'd first looked up and seen them. The other Jedi must all be dead.

"Master Windu!" Count Dooku's voice rang through the arena. "You have fought gallantly. You are worthy of recognition in the history archives of the Jedi Order. Now it is finished." He paused, then went on. "Surrender — and your lives will be spared."

"We will not be hostages for you to barter with,

Dooku." Mace Windu's deep voice was firm, though he had to know what Dooku's reaction would be.

"Then I'm sorry, old friend," Count Dooku said. "You will have to be destroyed." He raised his hand, and the Battle Droids raised their weapons.

"Look!" Padmé shouted. Obi-Wan glanced quickly around, confused; he saw nothing but Battle Droids. Then he realized that Padmé was pointing upward. He tilted his head back and saw six gunships drop through the open air above the arena.

The gunships landed in a ring between the tiny circle of Jedi and the Geonosian Battle Droids. The arena filled with harsh white light as the thousands of Battle Droids and Super Battle Droids fired their lasers — and the bolts bounced off the shields of the gunships. Obi-Wan stared in disbelief and wonder. *Who are they? Where did they come from?*

And then troops in white body armor came pouring out of the ships, and he knew. *The clone army! But how . . . ?* The clone troopers poured rapid, deadly fire on the droids, forcing them back.

Master Yoda appeared in the doorway of one of the gunships and motioned to the stunned Jedi. "Hurry!" he called.

Everyone raced to the gunships. As he boarded the nearest ship, Obi-Wan glanced up at the archducal box. It was empty. He looked down and saw the clone boy, Jango Fett's son, near one wall.

The boy was kneeling beside the battered helmet his father had worn. *So Master Windu disposed of the bounty hunter,* Obi-Wan thought. He felt sorry for the boy and wondered what would become of him, but there was nothing he could do now.

We're not finished with this yet, he thought as the gunships rose out of the arena. *There are still all those Trade Federation Core Ships in the landing area.*

And then there's Count Dooku to deal with.

CHAPTER 14

Anakin knew the fight was not over, but he was glad to have a minute to rest. Padmé was safely aboard, and there were no Battle Droids within reach of his lightsaber. The white-armored troopers inside the gunship fired one last time at the few Battle Droids still standing in the arena. Then the gunship lifted, and they were outside at last.

Outside — but not out of the fight. In spite of himself, Anakin's hand clenched his borrowed lightsaber. A mass of Trade Federation Core Ships and droids covered the ground around the arena. *No wonder they kept coming like that!* Anakin thought dazedly. He had no idea there were so many of them.

But the Trade Federation ships were themselves attacked. Thousands of men in white battle armor were firing into the rows of ships; beyond, Anakin could see Republic Assault Ships landing and more men heading for the battle.

"Look!" Obi-Wan called from the other side of the gunship. "Over there!"

Anakin peered out the open side of the gunship. A Geonosian speeder was heading rapidly away from the battle. In the open cockpit was the black-clad figure of Count Dooku.

"It's Dooku!" Anakin turned to the gunship's pilot. "Go after him!"

The pilot nodded and the gunship began to turn. Suddenly something exploded below the ship. The vessel lurched sideways. Caught by surprise, Padmé fell toward the edge of the ship. Anakin grabbed for her, but he was off balance and too far away, and she tumbled out.

"Padmé!" he cried in horror, then called frantically to the pilot. "Put the ship down! Down!"

Obi-Wan ran foward. "Don't let your personal feelings get in the way," he told Anakin sternly. Turning to the pilot, he waved toward the fleeing Count Dooku and commanded, "Follow that speeder."

Anakin glared at Obi-Wan. "Lower the ship," he told the pilot.

The pilot's helmet swiveled from Anakin to Obi-Wan in confusion.

Obi-Wan didn't seem to notice; his eyes were fixed on Anakin. "Anakin, I can't take Dooku alone," he said. "I need you. And if we catch him, we can end this war right now. We have a job to do."

"I don't care," Anakin said. After all they'd been through, to lose Padmé now would be unbearable. "Put the ship *down*."

"You'll be expelled from the Jedi Order," Obi-Wan warned.

Anakin swallowed hard and looked back. Padmé had rolled to the bottom of a dune. The sand was soft; she might be all right. *She must be all right.* But he couldn't tell, and there were still Trade Federation Battle Droids nearby. "I can't leave her," he said softly.

"Come to your senses," Obi-Wan said sharply.

Anakin looked up, startled, and a little angered by his Master's tone. Then he saw Obi-Wan's eyes — full of compassion and understanding, but still unyielding. "What so you think the Senator would do if she were in your position?" Obi-Wan asked softly.

Anakin fought to deny the answer, but he could not. "She would do her duty," he said heavily. He turned away as Obi-Wan ordered the pilot back on course. He kept his eyes on the unmoving Padmé until she was completely out of sight.

They followed Dooku to a hangar tower. The gunship landed just long enough for Obi-Wan and Anakin to jump off, then it started back toward the main battle while the two Jedi headed inside. They found Dooku at a hangar control panel. A small, fast Solar Sailer ship sat in front of the hangar doors, ready for takeoff.

He's running away, Anakin thought. Anger filled

him. "You're going to pay for all the Jedi you killed today, Dooku!" he said as the Count looked up from the controls.

Obi-Wan drew his lightsaber. "We move in together," he said. "You, slowly on the —"

"No," Anakin said. The anger that filled him was changing, becoming like the hate-filled rage he had felt on Tatooine, in the Tusken Raider camp. If he waited, if he went slowly, he would lose control again. *I am a Jedi! I can't feel like this!* "I'm taking him now!"

"Anakin, no!" Obi-Wan shouted as Anakin started forward. Anakin almost hesitated. But Obi-Wan didn't know about Tatooine and the Tusken Raiders. Obi-Wan must never know. And the only way to keep him from seeing Anakin in the same mindless rage was for Anakin to charge *now*, while he still had control of himself.

Count Dooku smiled faintly as Anakin approached. Anakin raised his lightsaber — and felt a surge in the Force. Dooku thrust out his arm and Anakin was thrown violently into the air. He had a moment to realize bitterly that he had failed *again*, and then he slammed hard into the far wall of the hangar and lost consciousness.

As Anakin slumped to the ground at the foot of the wall, Obi-Wan reached out to the Force. To his relief, he sensed that Anakin was not seriously hurt. But he could not wait for his apprentice to recover; Count Dooku was already moving toward him.

"As you can see, my Jedi powers are far beyond yours," Dooku said conversationally.

"I don't think so," Obi-Wan replied. Alone, he knew he had little chance of winning against Dooku. Not only was Dooku a master swordsman, he was rested and fresh, while Obi-Wan was already weary from the fight at the arena. *But I have to try,* Obi-Wan thought. He raised his lightsaber.

Dooku smiled and parried the first cut easily. He barely needed to move to parry the second and third strokes as well. "Master Kenobi, you disappoint me," he said. "Yoda holds you in such high esteem."

He's trying to distract me. Grimly, Obi-Wan fought on. His exhaustion was starting to tell; his breath came in harsh gasps. He backed off, hoping for a respite.

"Come, come, Master Kenobi," Count Dooku taunted. "Put me out of my misery."

Taking a deep breath, Obi-Wan shifted his grip and dove into the battle once more. Dooku gave ground, surprised by the ferocity of the attack, and for a moment Obi-Wan hoped that he might defeat the Count after all. But even drawing on the Force for strength, he was too tired to keep up the pace for long. The Count began to drive him back.

As Obi-Wan gave ground, Dooku quickened the

pace. His every move was economical and elegant; his lightsaber seemed to be everywhere. Obi-Wan remembered Jocasta Nu telling him, *With a lightsaber, in the old style of fencing, he had no match.* Now he could see what she meant. Unfortunately.

Obi-Wan missed a parry, and Dooku's lightsaber flashed into his shoulder. The pain was incredible. His lightsaber slowed a fatal fraction, and the Count's weapon hummed out and sliced his thigh.

The leg gave, and Obi-Wan stumbled back against the wall. His lightsaber dropped from his hand and went sliding away across the floor. He saw the Count raise his arm for the final blow, and he braced himself.

Count Dooku brought his weapon down — against a brilliant bar of blue light. Anakin stood over Obi-Wan, his face a mask of grim determination, his lightsaber forcing Dooku's back, away from his Master.

"That's brave of you, boy," Dooku said calmly. "But foolish. I would have thought you'd learned your lesson."

"I'm a slow learner," Anakin said, and charged.

To Obi-Wan's surprise, Anakin's attack caught the Count off balance and forced him back. The Count looked just as surprised as Obi-Wan, but he recovered quickly.

"You have unusual powers, young Padawan,"

Dooku said to Anakin. "But not enough to save you this time."

"Don't bet on it!" Anakin said.

But Dooku is right, Obi-Wan thought through the haze of pain and exhaustion. *Anakin is no match for him . . . unless Anakin does something unexpected.* Using all his remaining strength, he reached out with the Force. "Anakin!" he called, and flung his lightsaber to his apprentice.

Anakin caught the weapon in his free hand and attacked again. But even with two lightsabers, he could not hold back Count Dooku for long. The Count smiled and began to toy with him, knocking the extra lightsaber out of Anakin's hand.

Retreat, Obi-Wan thought. *Stall him.* But Anakin was not retreating; he was being driven back. The combat had almost come full circle, back to where Obi-Wan lay. The Count smiled slightly — Obi-Wan was not sure at whom — and his blade flicked out almost too fast to see. Anakin screamed as his right arm dropped to the floor, cut off at the elbow. He fell beside Obi-Wan, curling up in agony. Dooku looked down at the two Jedi and moved in for the kill.

Yoda pressed the switch to open the hangar doors. The battle with the Trade Federation droids was nearly finished; they no longer needed him there. Here, he sensed, was where he should be.

The doors slid open reluctantly, and Yoda walked

inside. *Yes, needed here, I am*, he thought as he saw Count Dooku standing over the fallen figures of Obi-Wan and Anakin. He stopped just inside the hangar, waiting.

Count Dooku saw him and stepped away from Anakin and Obi-Wan. Yoda bent his head in acknowledgment and regret. "Count Dooku."

"Master Yoda." The Count's tone was almost scornful, but Yoda sensed an eagerness in him — eagerness, and something darker. Dooku face hardened as he went on, "You've interfered with our plans for the last time."

Plans of conquest, Yoda thought sadly. *But a Jedi seeks not power*. Truly, Dooku had left the path of the Jedi Order. He felt Dooku gathering power, and he bowed his head in shock and sorrow as he sensed the true source of the Count's increased ability. An instant later, Dooku raised his hands and sent a stream of deadly Force lightning toward him.

Yoda blocked the lightning automatically, grieved by this final evidence of Dooku's change in allegiance. Only those who turned to the dark side of the Force misused their abilities so. This he had feared ever since Count Dooku left the Jedi Order, but only now was he certain. His old student had not just left the path of the Jedi; he had betrayed everything he had once stood for. He had joined the dark side. "Much to learn you still have," Yoda told him.

A startled expression crossed Dooku's face at the

utter failure of his attack. Then his eyes narrowed. He lowered his hands and replied, "It is obvious that this contest will not be decided by our knowledge of the Force, but by our skills with the lightsaber." As he spoke, he reignited his weapon and whirled it in the formal salute that Yoda remembered teaching him some fifty years before.

Yoda drew his lightsaber and answered the salute. In contests, he had no interest, but in stopping Count Dooku, he had a great deal of interest indeed. And Dooku had left him no other choice.

Count Dooku charged forward. Yoda sighed. *Nothing has he learned. Nothing has he remembered.* He closed his eyes, bowed his head, and felt the Force that bound all things, even himself and the Count. His lightsaber moved effortlessly, flowing with the Force to find the balance point between them and block Dooku's every stroke. He did not even have to step back.

The Count's attack grew more desperate, to no avail. Breathing hard, he backed away, but Yoda did not pursue him. To stop Dooku was all that was necessary, and he could not pass Yoda to reach his Solar Sailer.

The Count slowed once more, then stopped, his blade braced against Yoda's. Yoda could feel him drawing on the dark side in an attempt to press Yoda's weapon back, but the dark side was only an easier path, not a stronger one. Backed by the full power of the true Force, Yoda's lightsaber was unmovable.

"Fought well, you have, my old Padawan," Yoda said gently, giving him the truth, though he knew that the Count would not want to hear it. Count Dooku had never been happy to merely fight *well*; the *best* he must be, always. But not this time.

"This is just the beginning," the Count snarled.

Yoda felt a great surge in the Force as Count Dooku pulled one of the service cranes off balance. The mass of metal and wire plummeted directly toward Obi-Wan and Anakin. Yoda could feel the two exhausted, injured Jedi reaching for the Force to keep the crane from falling, but they did not have enough strength left. The falling crane slowed but did not stop; it would surely crush them when it landed.

No decision was necessary. *Too many Jedi have we lost today.* Yoda bent his mind toward the crane, concentrating. The crane stopped abruptly in midair as if it had landed on some invisible table. Slowly, Yoda moved the crane away from Obi-Wan and Anakin, to an empty part of the hangar where it could settle safely to the ground.

Behind him, he sensed the engines of the Solar Sailer start, then felt them fade into the distance. The Count had escaped. But Anakin and Obi-Wan were still alive.

For now, that was enough.

CHAPTER 15

Cautiously, Count Dooku's Solar Sailer approached Coruscant. The Count was in no hurry. The important thing was to avoid detection, and he'd had plenty of practice at that. He was sure he wouldn't be late for his meeting. He had allowed himself plenty of time.

The ship slid through Coruscant's warning systems without triggering them, and glided down toward the surface of the planet. The Count steered toward a burned-out section that had been abandoned eight years before. It was still deserted, and it made a perfect place for him to slip in and out of Coruscant unnoticed.

Dooku flew toward one of the buildings and landed inside, out of sight. As he lowered the ramp, he saw a hooded figure waiting in the shadows. *He always knows,* the Count thought. *But then, he should. That is why he is the Master.*

Leaving his ship, Dooku crossed to the waiting figure. He bowed low. "The Force is with us, Master Sidious."

His Master lowered his head briefly in acknowledgment. "Welcome home, Lord Tyranus," Darth Sidious said in his precise, whispery voice. "You have done well."

"I bring you good news, my Lord," Dooku said. Though he knew that everyone on Coruscant must already have heard, his instructions had been to return here with the news — and Darth Sidious had a short and unpleasant way with anyone who disobeyed even the smallest part of his orders. "The war has begun."

"Excellent." Sidious's dry voice sounded almost enthusiastic, and his lips — the only part of him visible beneath the deep hood — curved in a slight smile. "Everything is going as planned."

Count Dooku returned the smile. *Darth Sidious plans well, and carefully. Soon we two will rule the galaxy.*

Soon.

Obi-Wan stood beside Mace Windu, staring out the window at the great plaza below the Jedi Temple. Yoda sat nearby in his Council chair. It was good to be home, Obi-Wan thought, but Coruscant felt different now. Clone troopers in their smooth white body armor were everywhere. The Senate thought that their presence made people feel safe, but to

Obi-Wan they were only a reminder of the vicious battle on Geonosis and all the Jedi who had not returned from it.

Bacta treatments had mended both his wounds and Anakin's, though even that powerful healing agent could not regrow Anakin's arm. Anakin would have to make do with a mechanical replacement. He wouldn't be the first Jedi to have to do so. *And he probably won't be the last,* Obi-Wan thought somberly. Count Dooku had gotten clean away; he would undoubtedly make more trouble.

The thought brought to mind some of the things the Count had told him, and he turned to Master Windu. "Do you believe what Count Dooku said about Sidious controlling the Senate?" he asked. "It doesn't feel right."

"Become unreliable, Dooku has," Yoda said before Mace could reply. His voice dropped. "Joined the dark side. Lies, deceit, creating mistrust are his ways now."

Master Windu held up a hand. "Nevertheless, I feel we should keep a closer eye on the Senate."

Yoda nodded. "I agree."

Mace Windu turned back to Obi-Wan. "Where is your apprentice?"

"On his way to Naboo," Obi-Wan said. "He is escorting Senator Amidala home." Anakin had told him of Shmi's death; that was why he and Padmé had gone to Tatooine, he said. Obi-Wan had talked to Padmé later, and she had explained that Shmi had been kidnapped and killed by Tusken Raiders.

Neither of them had been willing to go into much detail, and from what Obi-Wan knew of the Tusken Raiders, he didn't blame them. It was no wonder Anakin seemed shaken, if his mother had been tortured and killed. One day, perhaps, Anakin would be willing to tell him the whole story. In the meantime, Padmé's presence seemed to cheer Anakin up, and it would be good for Anakin to spend a little time on a beautiful planet like Naboo. It might take his mind off the horror of his mother's death, and of the battle on Geonosis.

They had lost so many Jedi. Two hundred had gone to Geonosis; barely twenty had returned. Still, they had won. "I have to admit, without the clones it would not have been a victory," Obi-Wan said.

"Victory?" Yoda sat indignantly upright in his chair. "Victory, you say?"

Obi-Wan turned. Yoda looked around the almost-empty Council chamber, and his ears drooped sadly. "Master Obi-Wan, not victory," he said softly. "Only begun, this Clone War has."

The words rang in Obi-Wan's head. He closed his eyes, remembering the endless lines of clone troopers on Kamino. They were on Coruscant now — tens of thousands of clones, boarding Republic Assault

Ships that would take them to fight on the Separatist worlds. There were many times as many troopers as there were Jedi, and the Kaminoans had a million more on the way. *It takes more beings to fight a war than it does to keep the peace,* Obi-Wan thought gloomily, and realized that Yoda was right. The war had only begun.

If Padmé had ever thought about her wedding, she had pictured a formal ceremony with her family and friends as witnesses. She had never, in her wildest dreams, expected to be married secretly on an isolated island with only a pair of droids to watch the Holy Man's blessing. But she was here, and she could imagine no more perfect place to marry Anakin than the balcony of this lake lodge where she had begun to discover her love for him. The roses in the garden below were past their prime, shedding petals at the slightest breeze. The fading flowers drenched the air with their perfume.

Anakin seemed serious, almost sad, as they exchanged their vows, and for a moment Padmé wondered if they were doing the right thing. But it was too late to change her mind now; the vows were spoken.

The Holy Man blessed them, and Anakin turned to smile down at her. Padmé smiled back, trying to set her misgivings aside. He raised his hand to her shoulder — his right hand, the one that was now only a clever mechanical imitation of a real arm. Was it only her imagination, or were the wires and metal too cool against her neck?

Anakin's blue eyes darkened and his smile faded slightly. Did he sense the doubts she had tried to hide, or was it his own uncertainty she saw in his eyes? *It would destroy us,* he had said, and he had sounded so sure, as if he knew. But he had lost so much; surely he didn't have to lose this, too. *Not doing this would destroy us, too,* Padmé thought. *We'll make it work. Somehow.*

Then Anakin bent and kissed her, and she had no more doubts. There was only Anakin, and the scent of the dying roses in the garden below.